TOMMI PARRISH

THE LIE AND HOW WE TOLD IT

FANTAGRAPHICS BOOKS

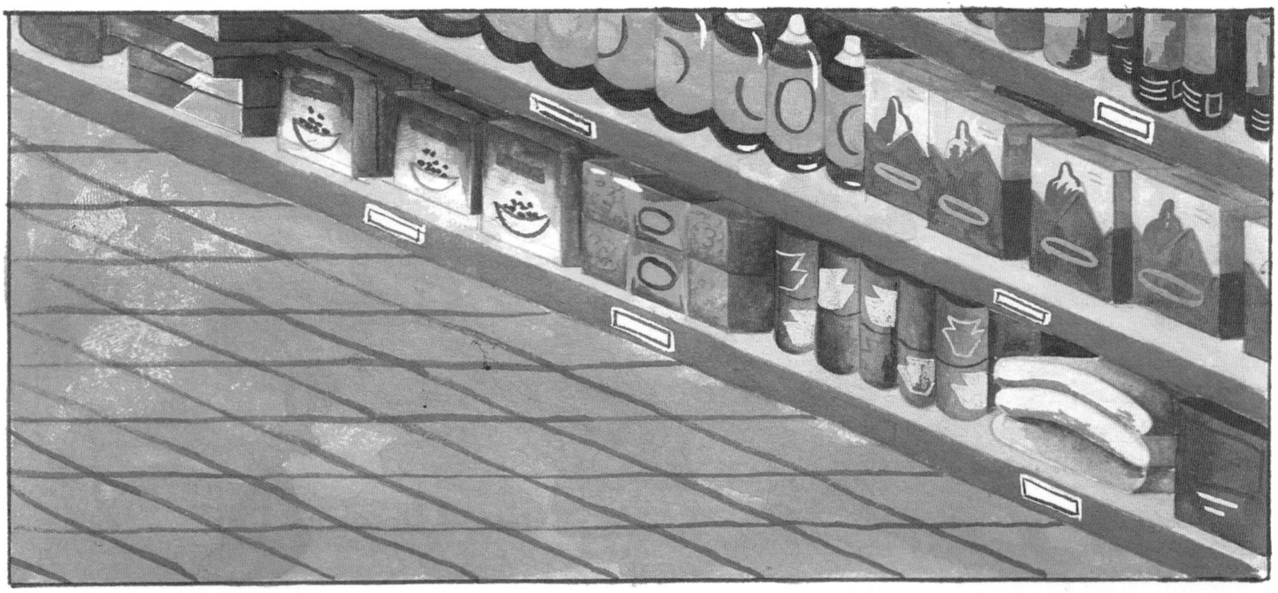

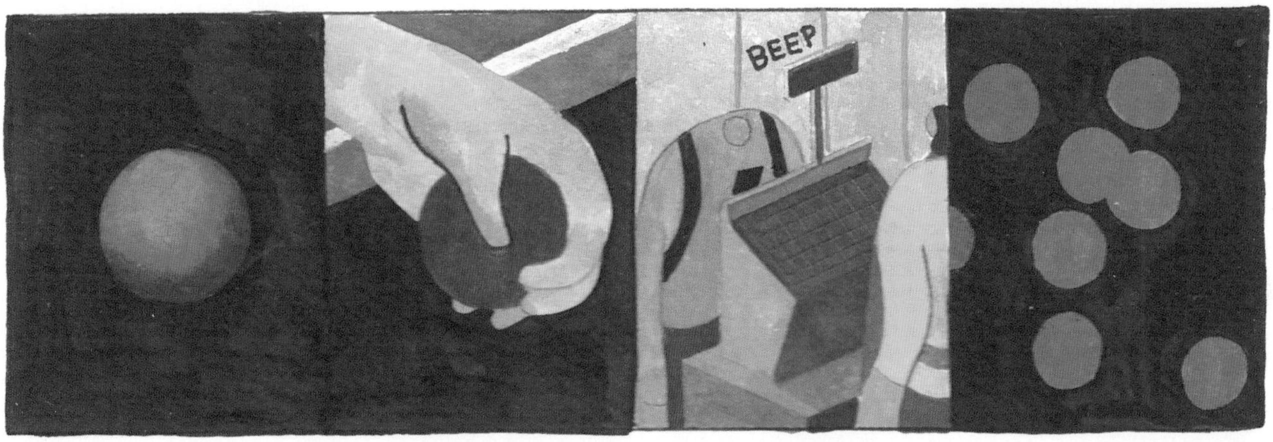
BEEP

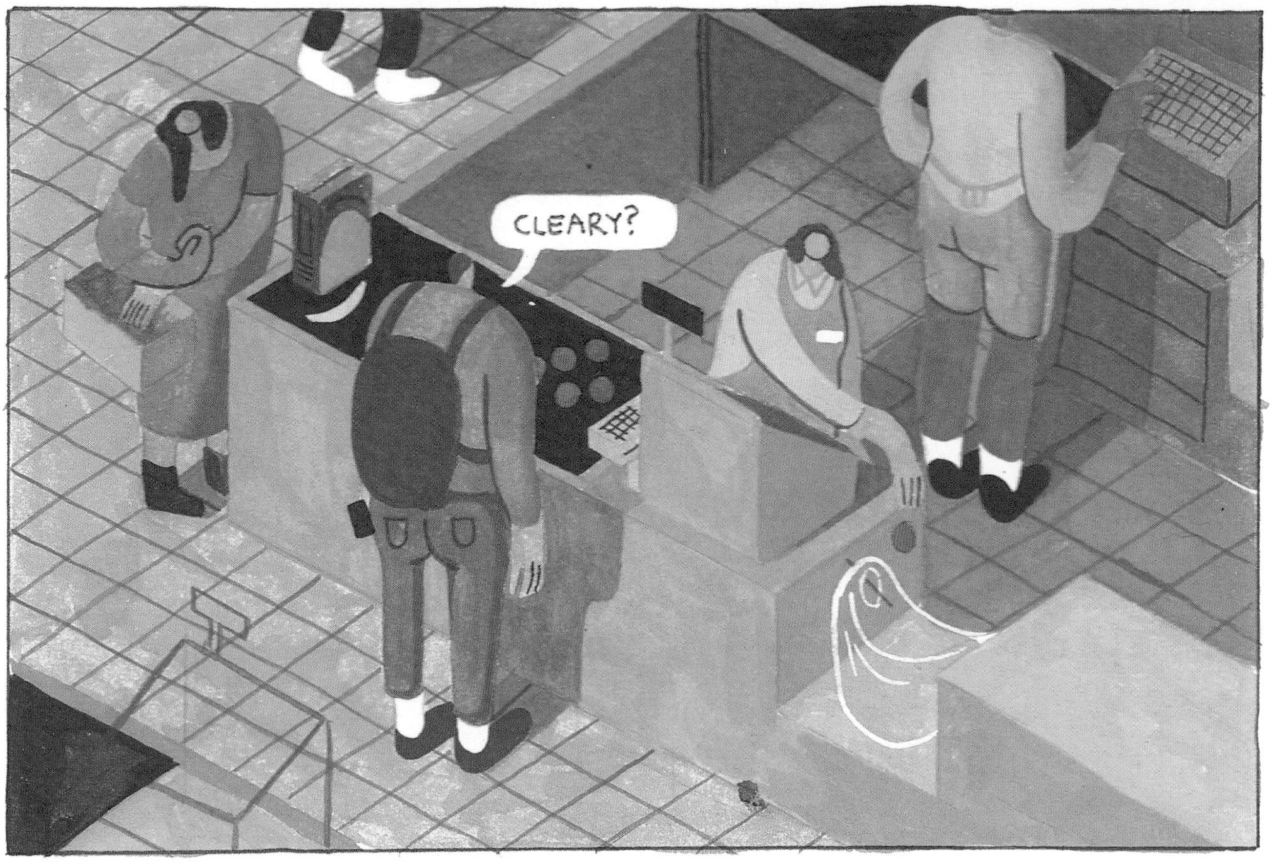
CLEARY?

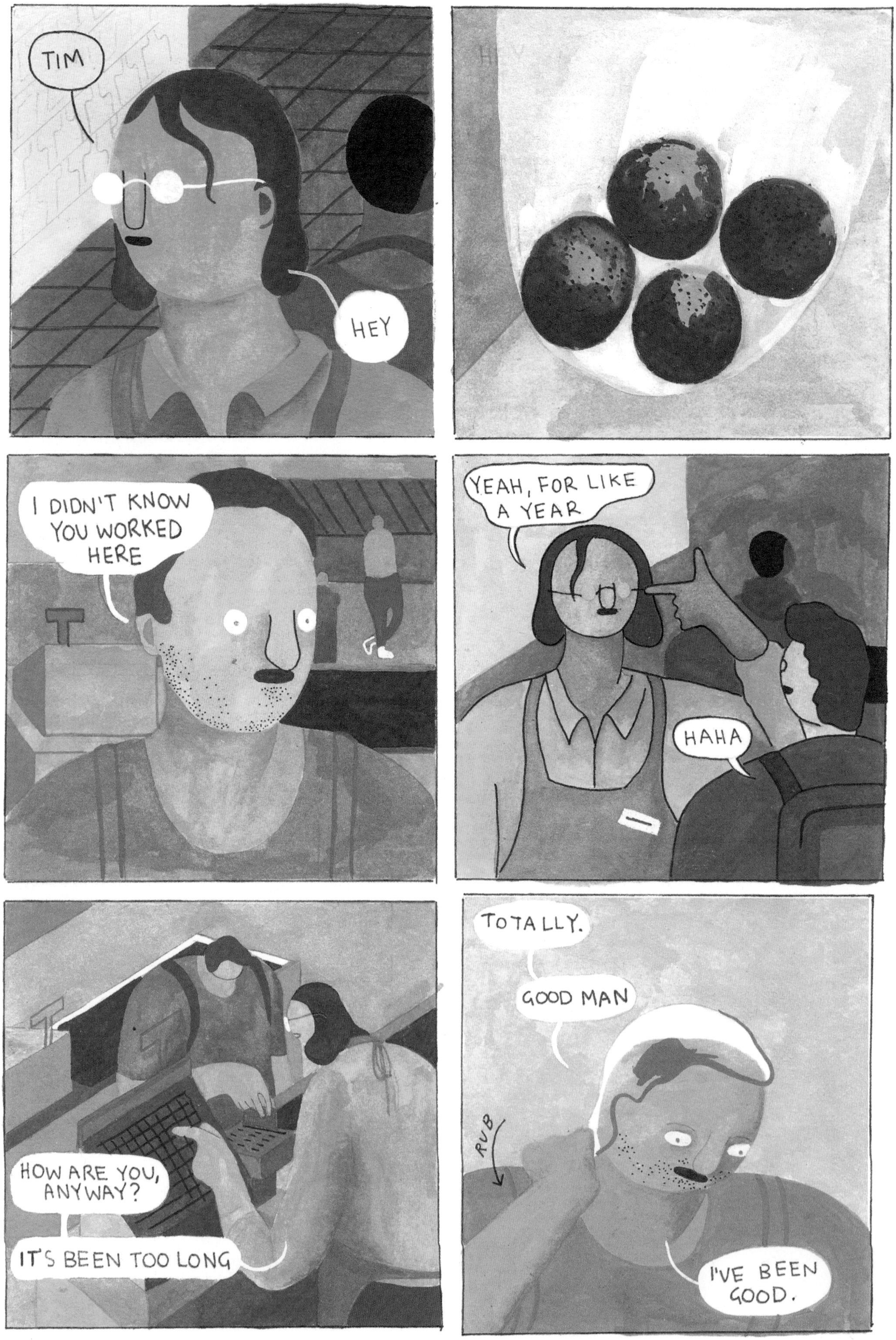
TIM
HEY
I DIDN'T KNOW YOU WORKED HERE
YEAH, FOR LIKE A YEAR
HAHA
HOW ARE YOU, ANYWAY?
IT'S BEEN TOO LONG
TOTALLY.
GOOD MAN
RUB
I'VE BEEN GOOD.

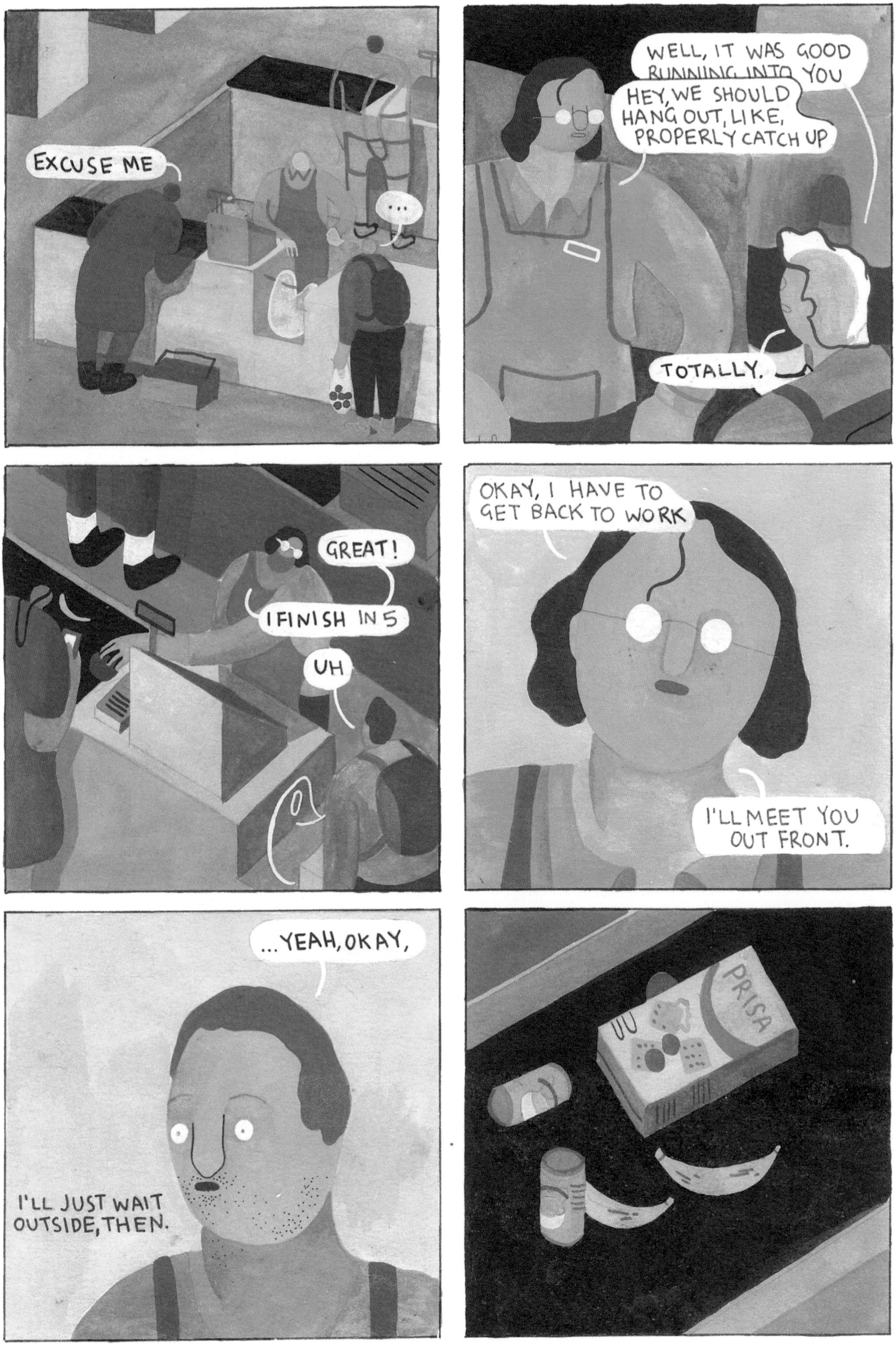
EXCUSE ME
...
WELL, IT WAS GOOD RUNNING INTO YOU
HEY, WE SHOULD HANG OUT, LIKE, PROPERLY CATCH UP
TOTALLY.
GREAT!
I FINISH IN 5
UH
OKAY, I HAVE TO GET BACK TO WORK
I'LL MEET YOU OUT FRONT.
...YEAH, OKAY,
I'LL JUST WAIT OUTSIDE, THEN.
PRISA

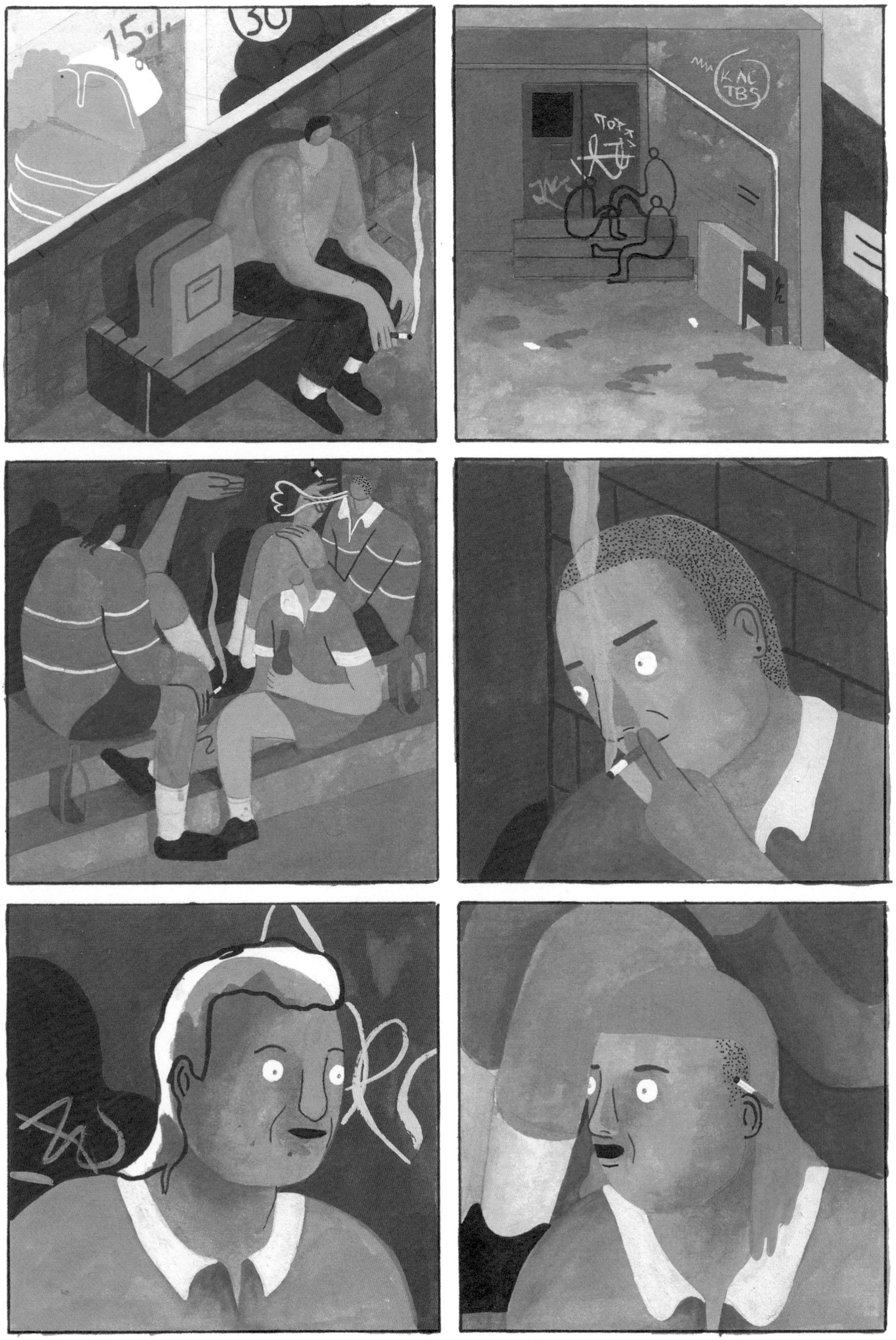
15%
30
KAC TBS

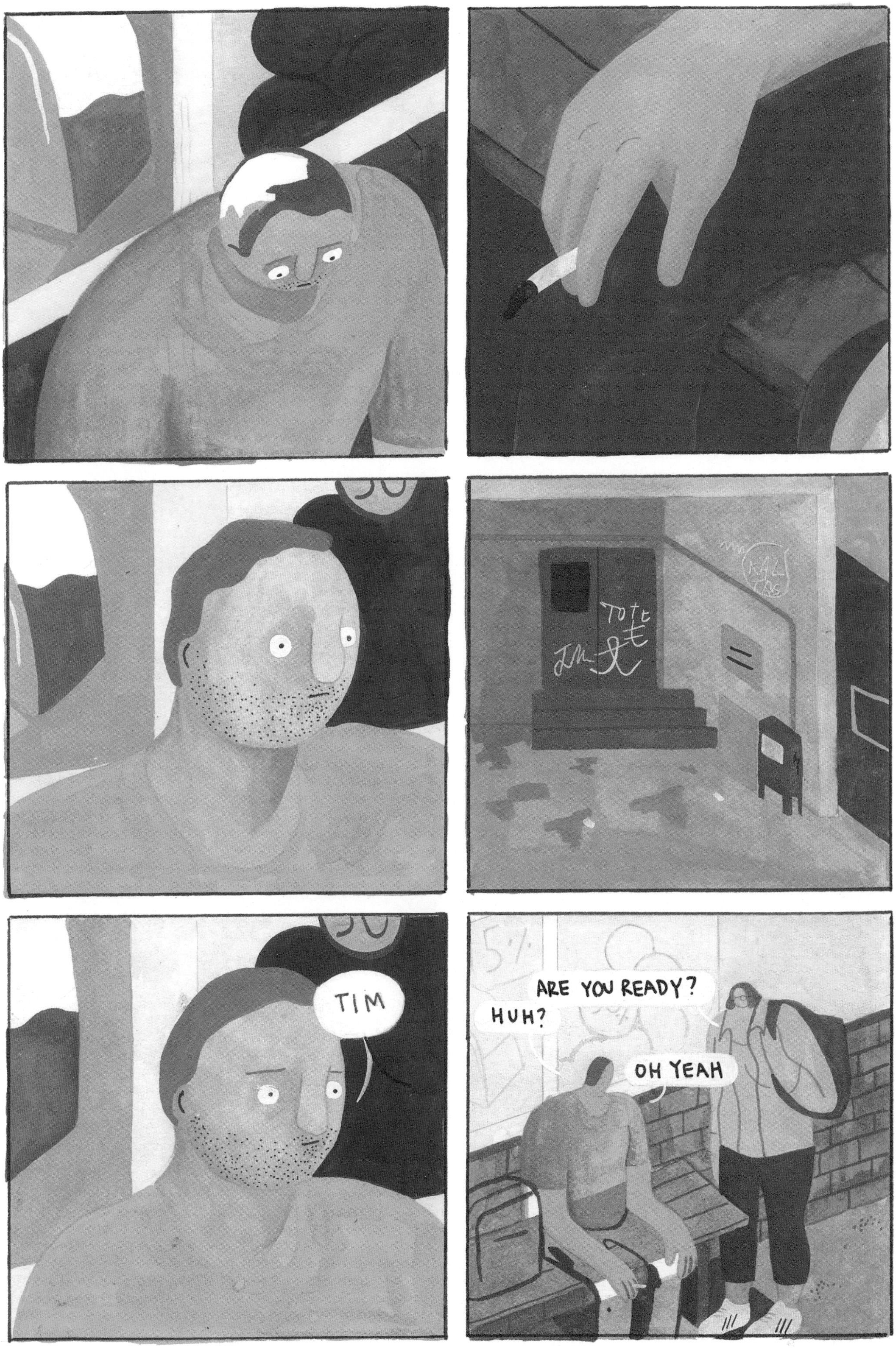
TIM
ARE YOU READY?
HUH?
OH YEAH

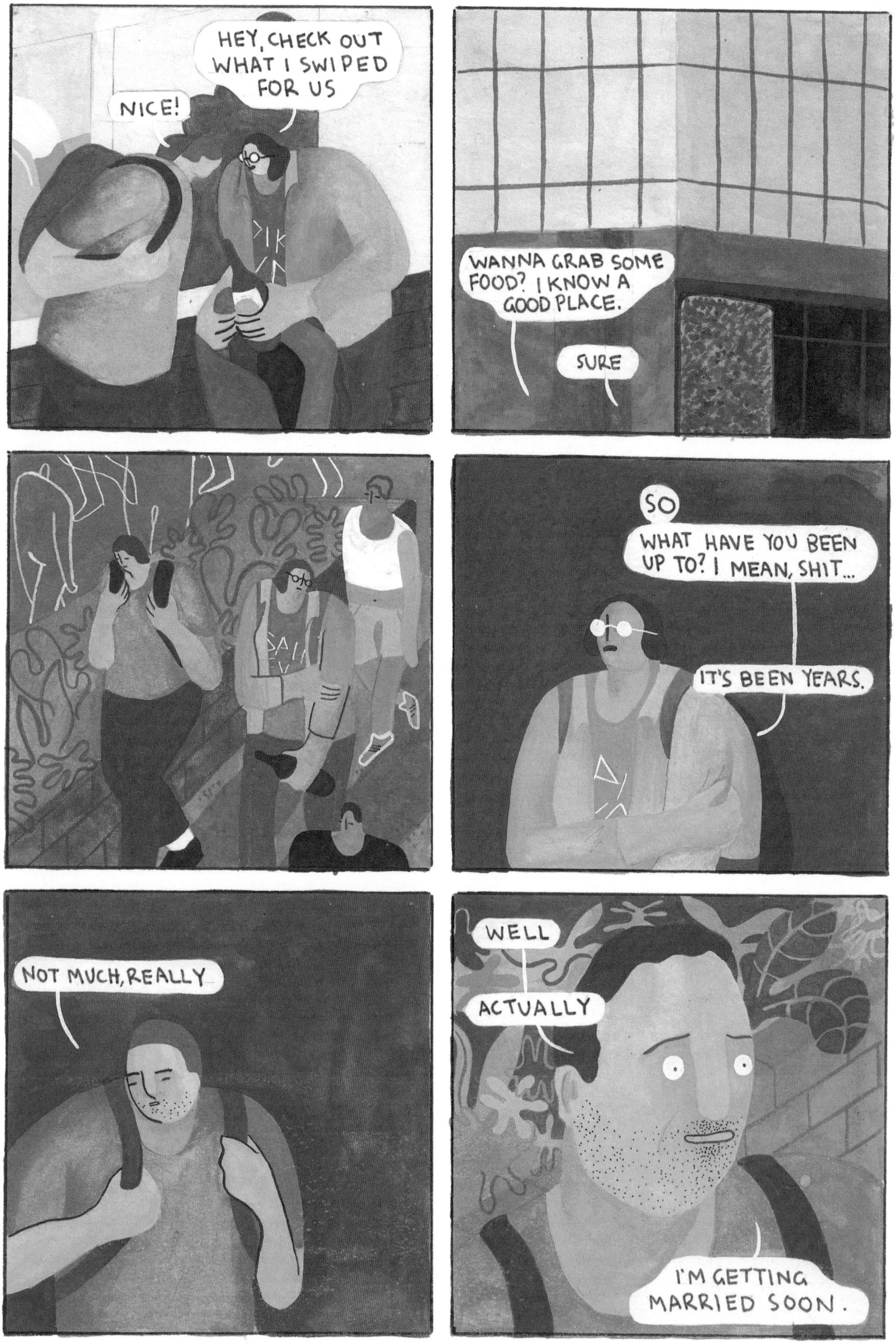
HEY, CHECK OUT WHAT I SWIPED FOR US
NICE!
WANNA GRAB SOME FOOD? I KNOW A GOOD PLACE.
SURE
SO
WHAT HAVE YOU BEEN UP TO? I MEAN, SHIT...
IT'S BEEN YEARS.
NOT MUCH, REALLY
WELL
ACTUALLY
I'M GETTING MARRIED SOON.

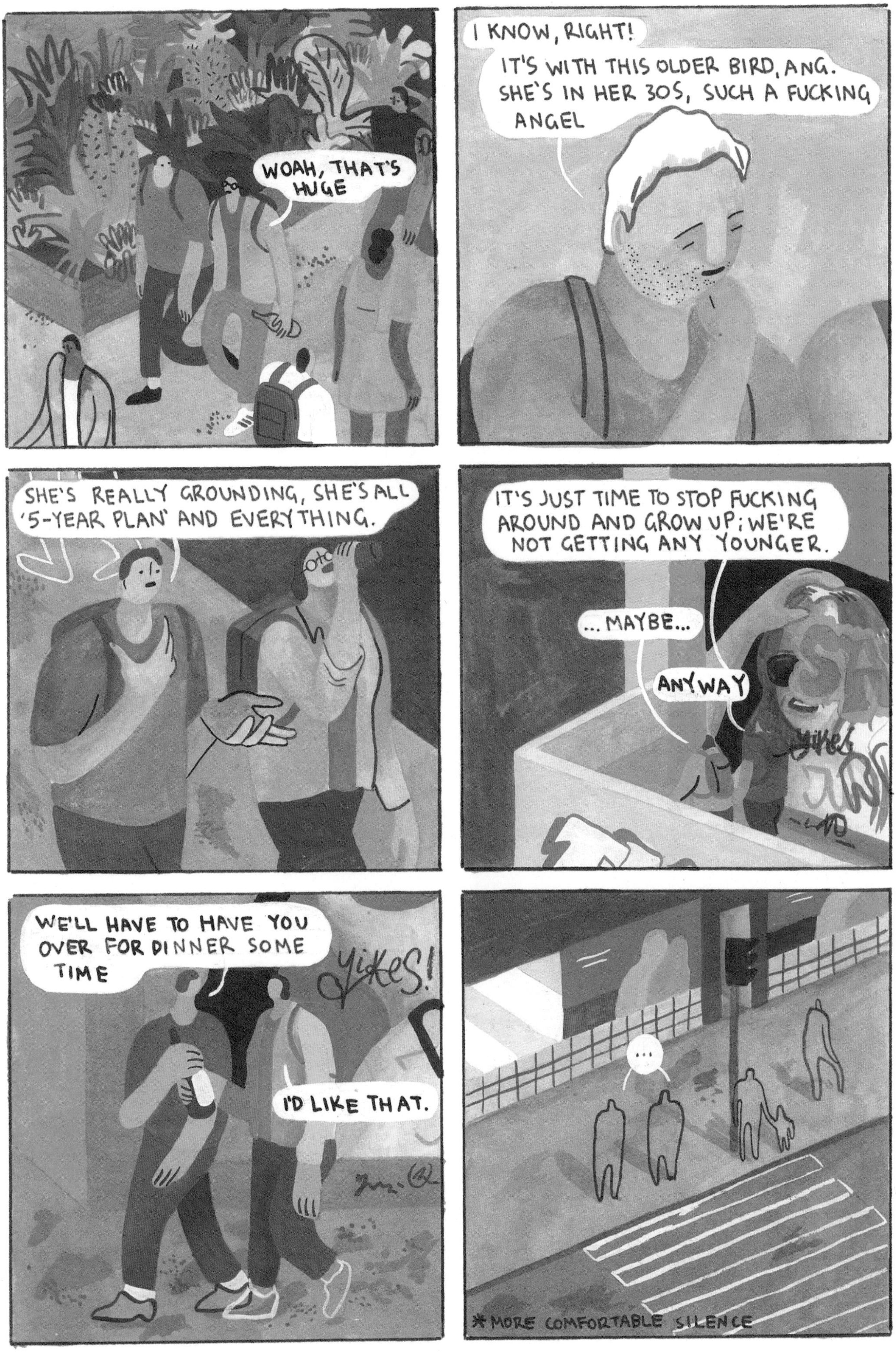
WOAH, THAT'S HUGE
I KNOW, RIGHT!
IT'S WITH THIS OLDER BIRD, ANG. SHE'S IN HER 30S, SUCH A FUCKING ANGEL
SHE'S REALLY GROUNDING, SHE'S ALL '5-YEAR PLAN' AND EVERYTHING.
IT'S JUST TIME TO STOP FUCKING AROUND AND GROW UP; WE'RE NOT GETTING ANY YOUNGER.
... MAYBE...
ANYWAY
WE'LL HAVE TO HAVE YOU OVER FOR DINNER SOME TIME
yikes!
I'D LIKE THAT.
...
*MORE COMFORTABLE SILENCE

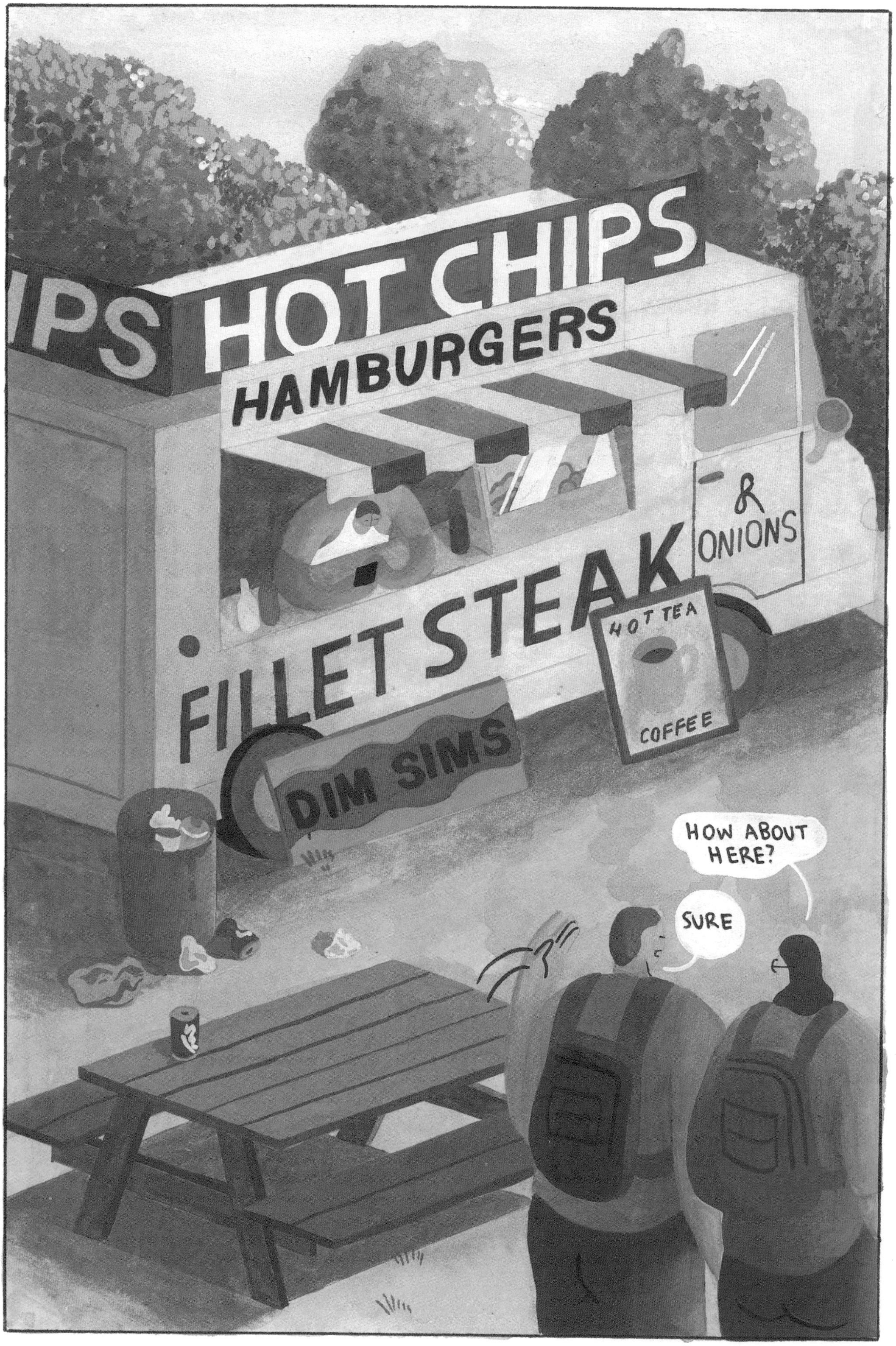
PS HOT CHIPS
HAMBURGERS
& ONIONS
FILLET STEAK
HOT TEA
COFFEE
DIM SIMS
HOW ABOUT HERE?
SURE

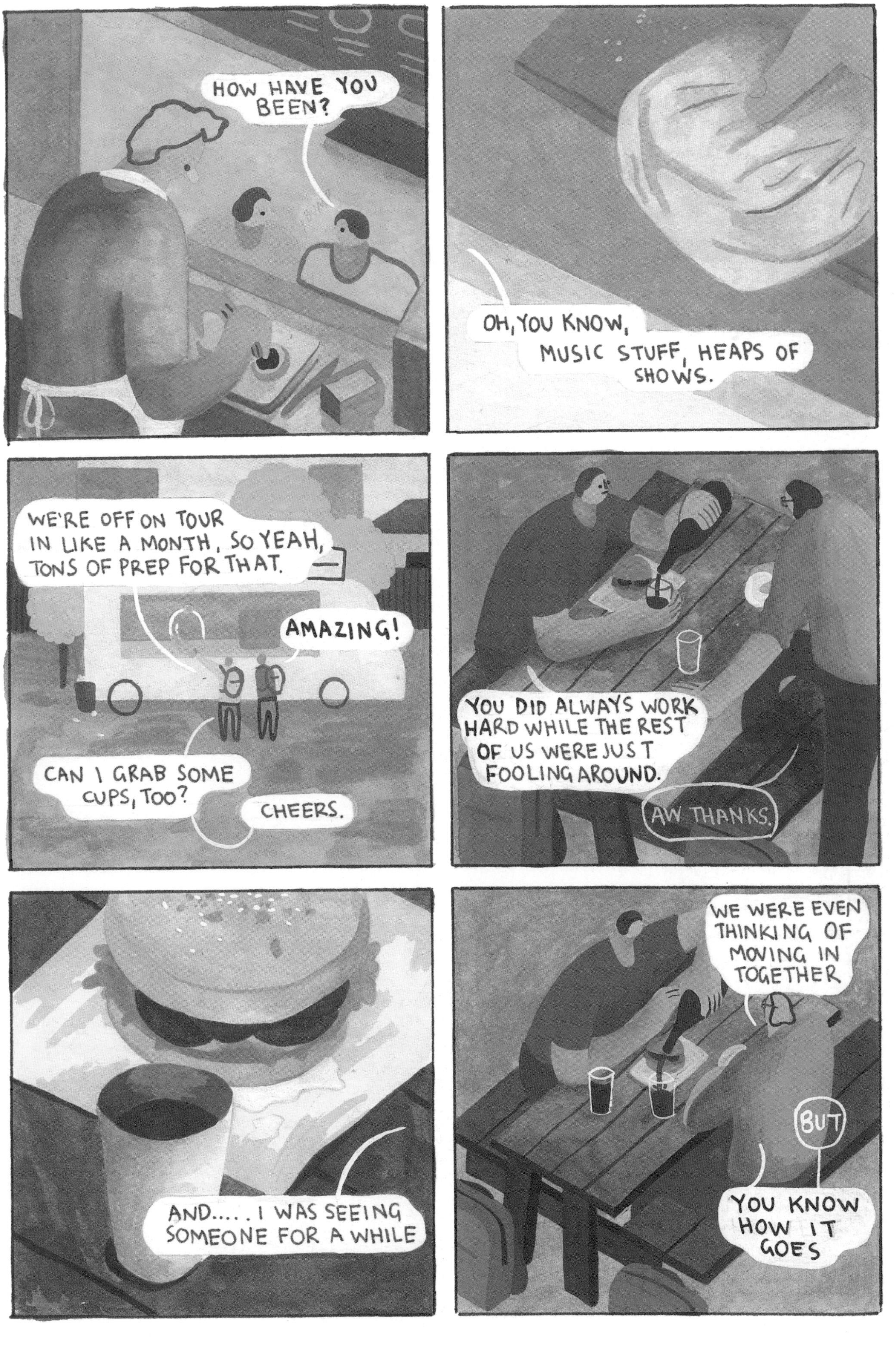
HOW HAVE YOU BEEN?
OH, YOU KNOW,
MUSIC STUFF, HEAPS OF SHOWS.
WE'RE OFF ON TOUR IN LIKE A MONTH, SO YEAH, TONS OF PREP FOR THAT.
AMAZING!
CAN I GRAB SOME CUPS, TOO?
CHEERS.
YOU DID ALWAYS WORK HARD WHILE THE REST OF US WERE JUST FOOLING AROUND.
AW THANKS.
AND..... I WAS SEEING SOMEONE FOR A WHILE
WE WERE EVEN THINKING OF MOVING IN TOGETHER
BUT
YOU KNOW HOW IT GOES

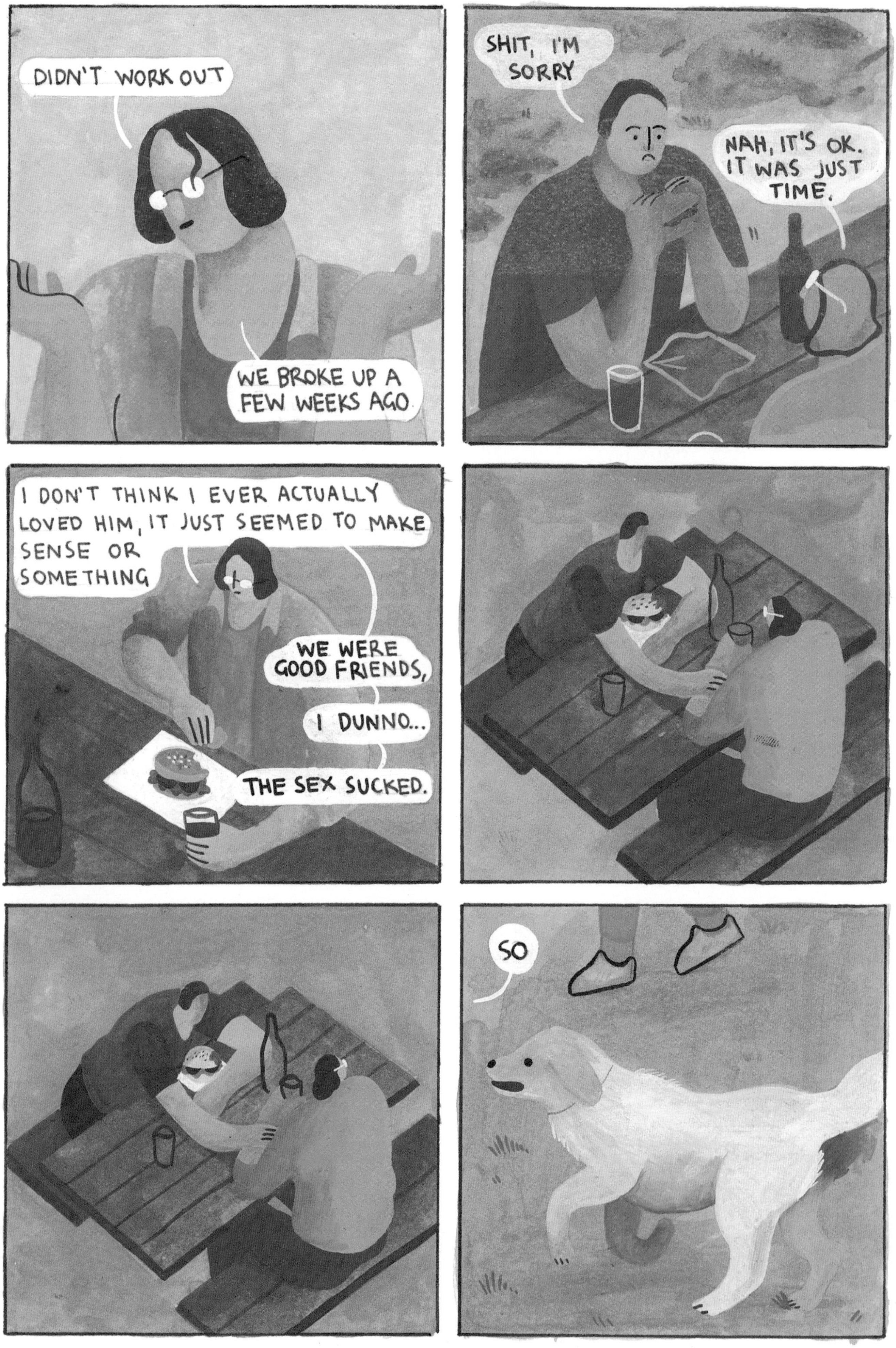
DIDN'T WORK OUT
WE BROKE UP A FEW WEEKS AGO
SHIT, I'M SORRY
NAH, IT'S OK. IT WAS JUST TIME.
I DON'T THINK I EVER ACTUALLY LOVED HIM, IT JUST SEEMED TO MAKE SENSE OR SOMETHING
WE WERE GOOD FRIENDS,
I DUNNO...
THE SEX SUCKED.
SO

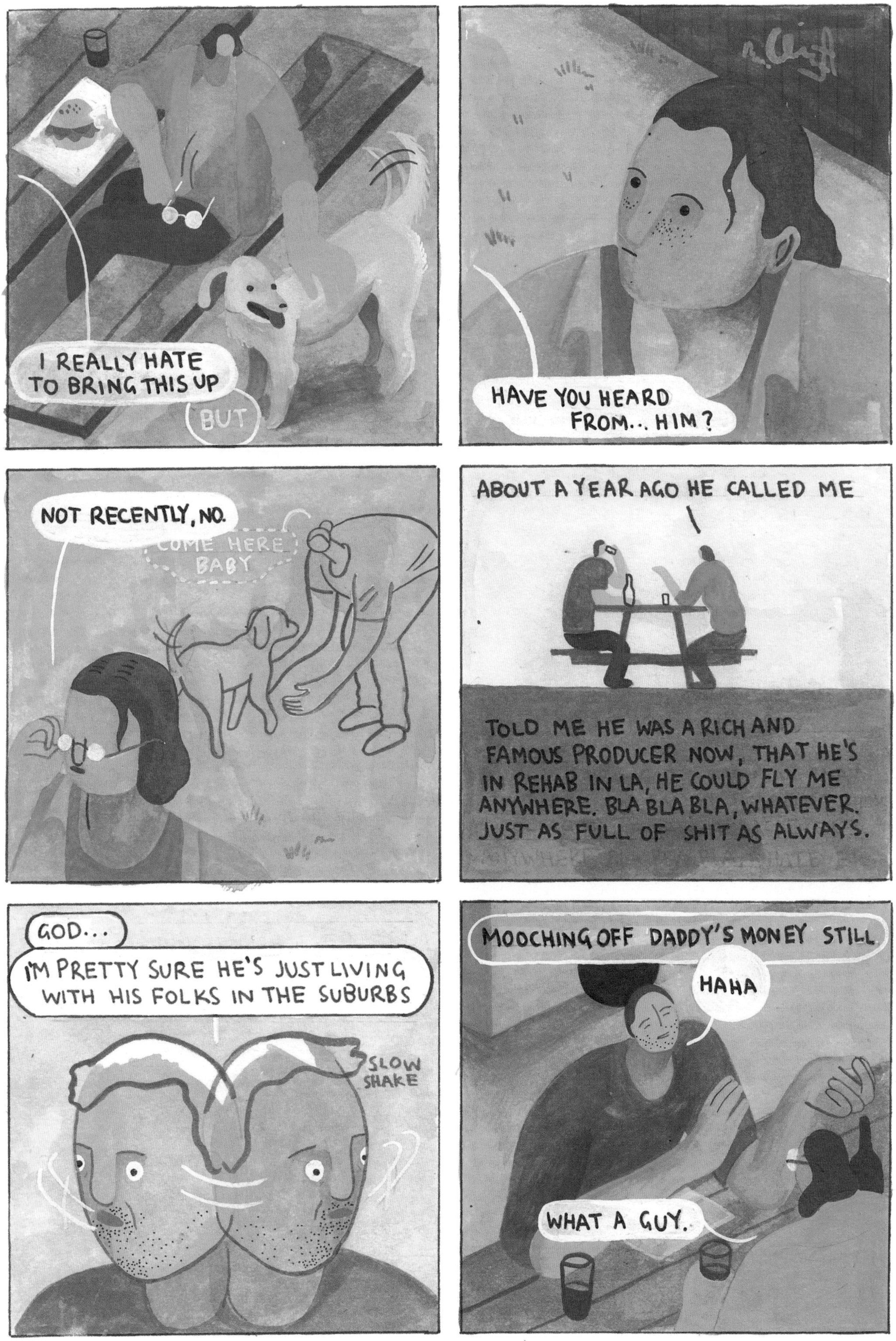
I REALLY HATE TO BRING THIS UP
BUT
HAVE YOU HEARD FROM... HIM?
NOT RECENTLY, NO.
COME HERE BABY
ABOUT A YEAR AGO HE CALLED ME
TOLD ME HE WAS A RICH AND FAMOUS PRODUCER NOW, THAT HE'S IN REHAB IN LA, HE COULD FLY ME ANYWHERE. BLA BLA BLA, WHATEVER. JUST AS FULL OF SHIT AS ALWAYS.
GOD...
I'M PRETTY SURE HE'S JUST LIVING WITH HIS FOLKS IN THE SUBURBS
SLOW SHAKE
MOOCHING OFF DADDY'S MONEY STILL
HAHA
WHAT A GUY.

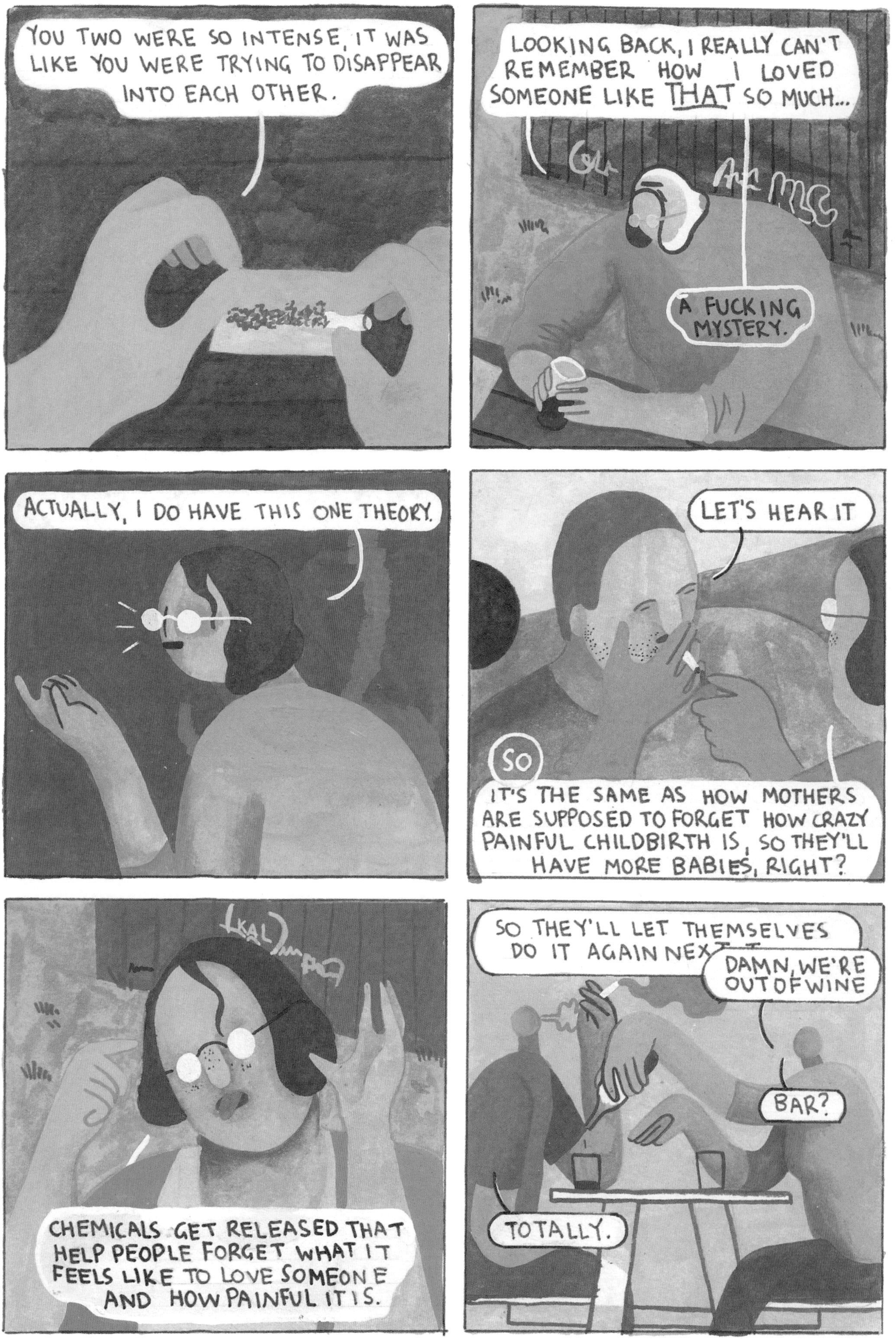
YOU TWO WERE SO INTENSE, IT WAS LIKE YOU WERE TRYING TO DISAPPEAR INTO EACH OTHER.
LOOKING BACK, I REALLY CAN'T REMEMBER HOW I LOVED SOMEONE LIKE THAT SO MUCH...
A FUCKING MYSTERY.
ACTUALLY, I DO HAVE THIS ONE THEORY.
LET'S HEAR IT
SO
IT'S THE SAME AS HOW MOTHERS ARE SUPPOSED TO FORGET HOW CRAZY PAINFUL CHILDBIRTH IS, SO THEY'LL HAVE MORE BABIES, RIGHT?
CHEMICALS GET RELEASED THAT HELP PEOPLE FORGET WHAT IT FEELS LIKE TO LOVE SOMEONE AND HOW PAINFUL IT IS.
SO THEY'LL LET THEMSELVES DO IT AGAIN NEX
DAMN, WE'RE OUT OF WINE
BAR?
TOTALLY.

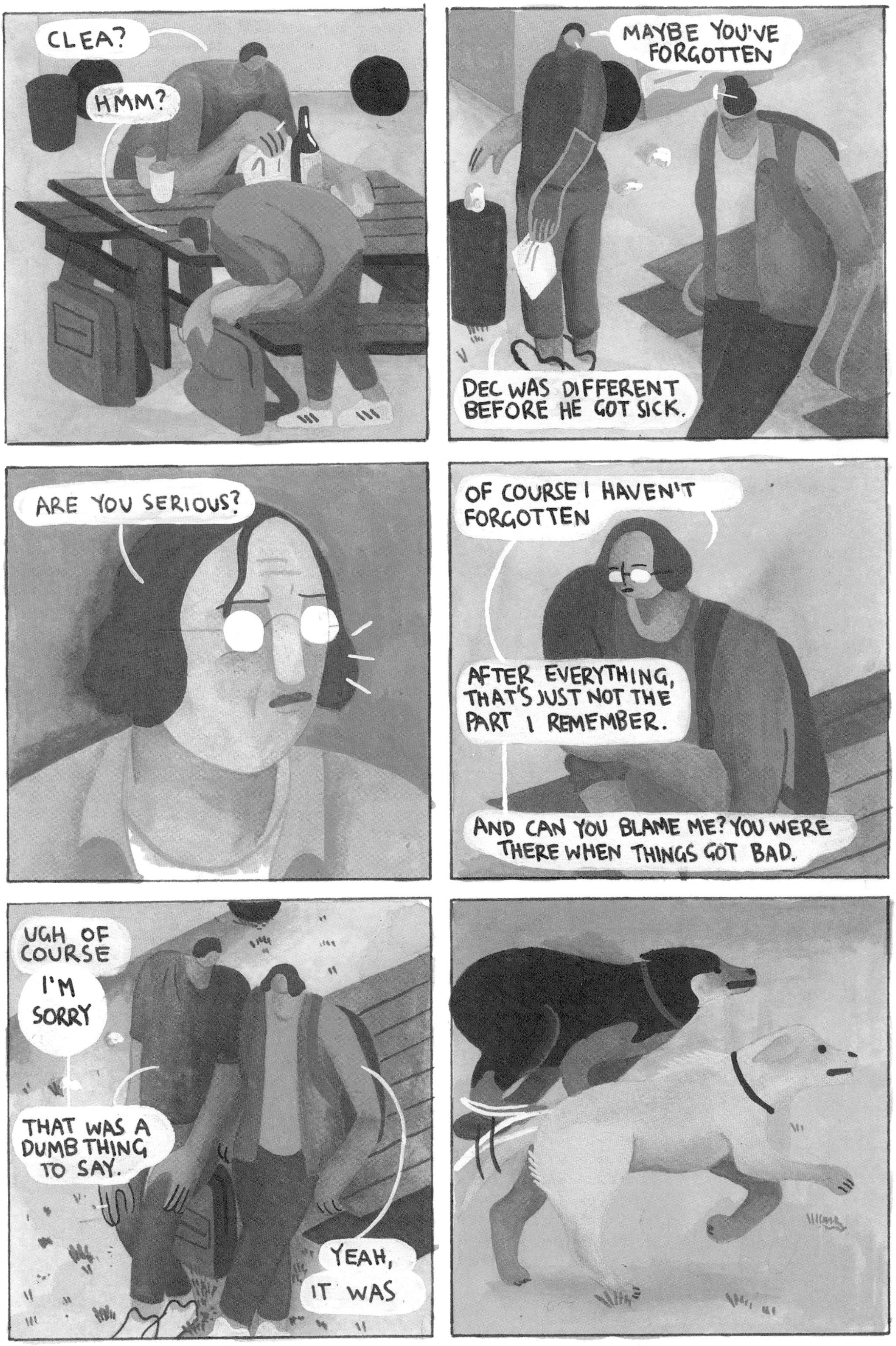
CLEA?
HMM?
MAYBE YOU'VE FORGOTTEN
DEC WAS DIFFERENT BEFORE HE GOT SICK.
ARE YOU SERIOUS?
OF COURSE I HAVEN'T FORGOTTEN
AFTER EVERYTHING, THAT'S JUST NOT THE PART I REMEMBER.
AND CAN YOU BLAME ME? YOU WERE THERE WHEN THINGS GOT BAD.
UGH OF COURSE
I'M SORRY
THAT WAS A DUMB THING TO SAY.
YEAH, IT WAS

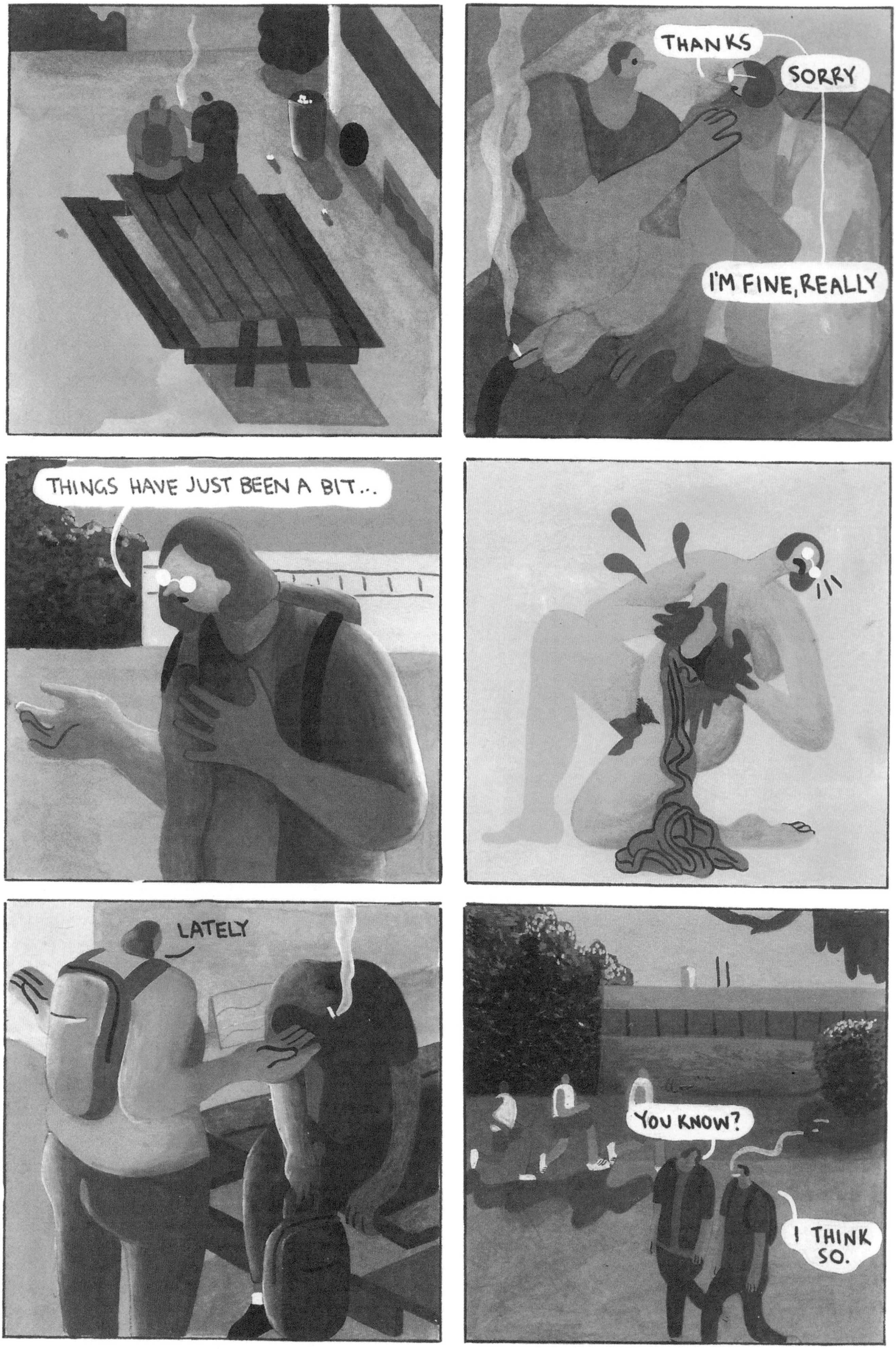
THANKS
SORRY
I'M FINE, REALLY
THINGS HAVE JUST BEEN A BIT...
LATELY
YOU KNOW?
I THINK SO.

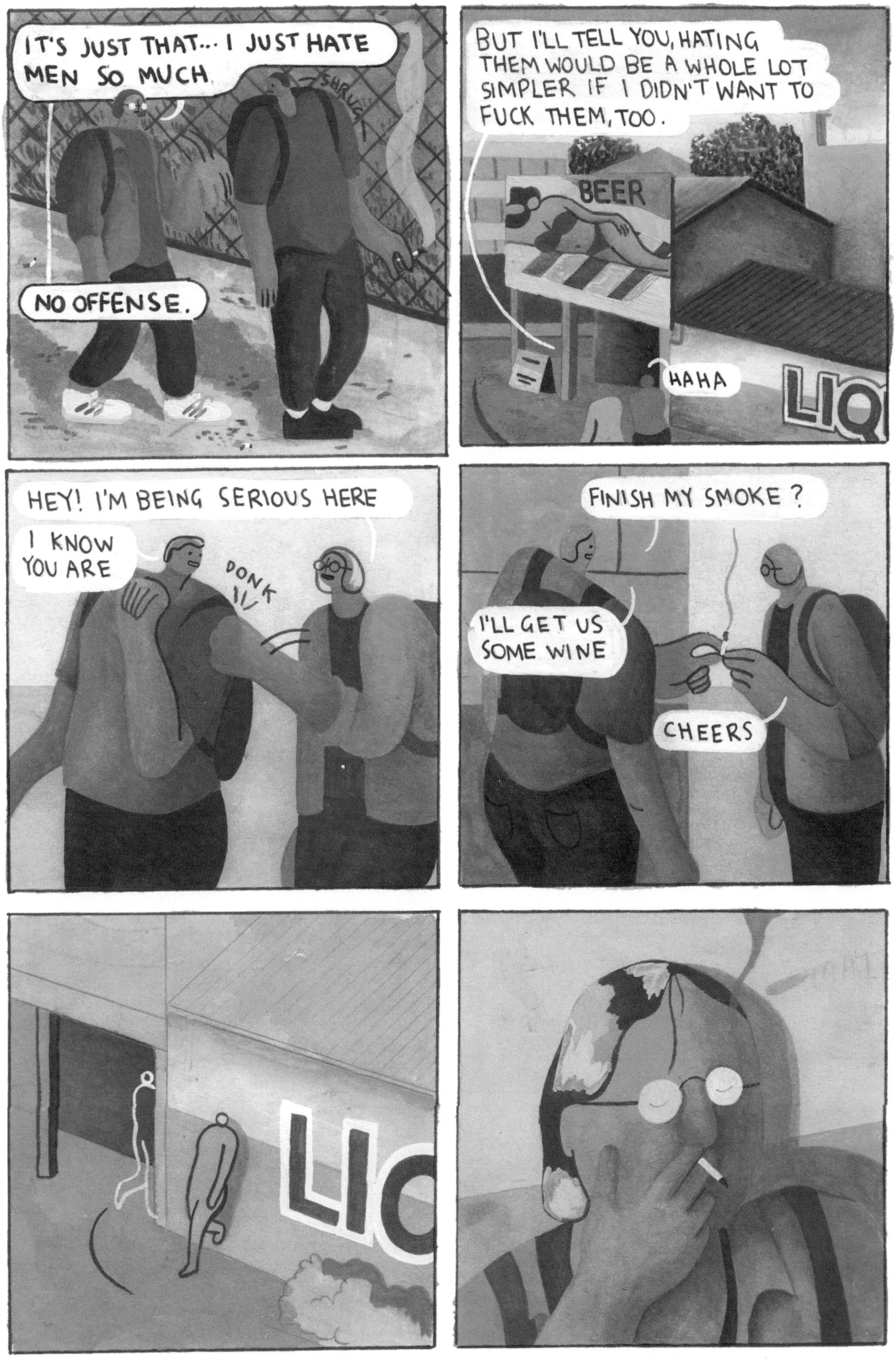
IT'S JUST THAT... I JUST HATE MEN SO MUCH
SHRUG
NO OFFENSE.
BUT I'LL TELL YOU, HATING THEM WOULD BE A WHOLE LOT SIMPLER IF I DIDN'T WANT TO FUCK THEM, TOO.
BEER
HAHA
LIQ
HEY! I'M BEING SERIOUS HERE
I KNOW YOU ARE
DONK
FINISH MY SMOKE?
I'LL GET US SOME WINE
CHEERS
LIQ

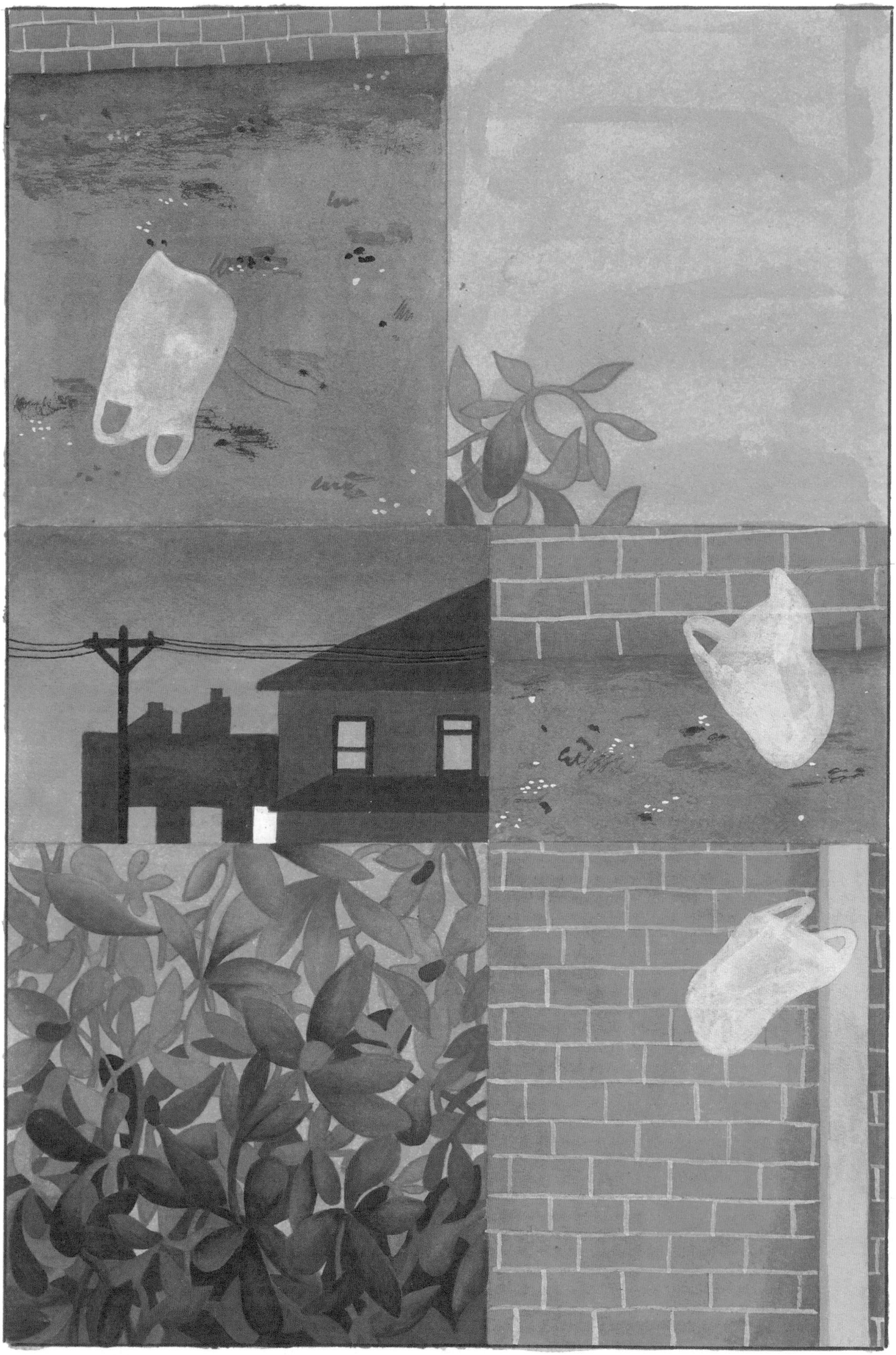

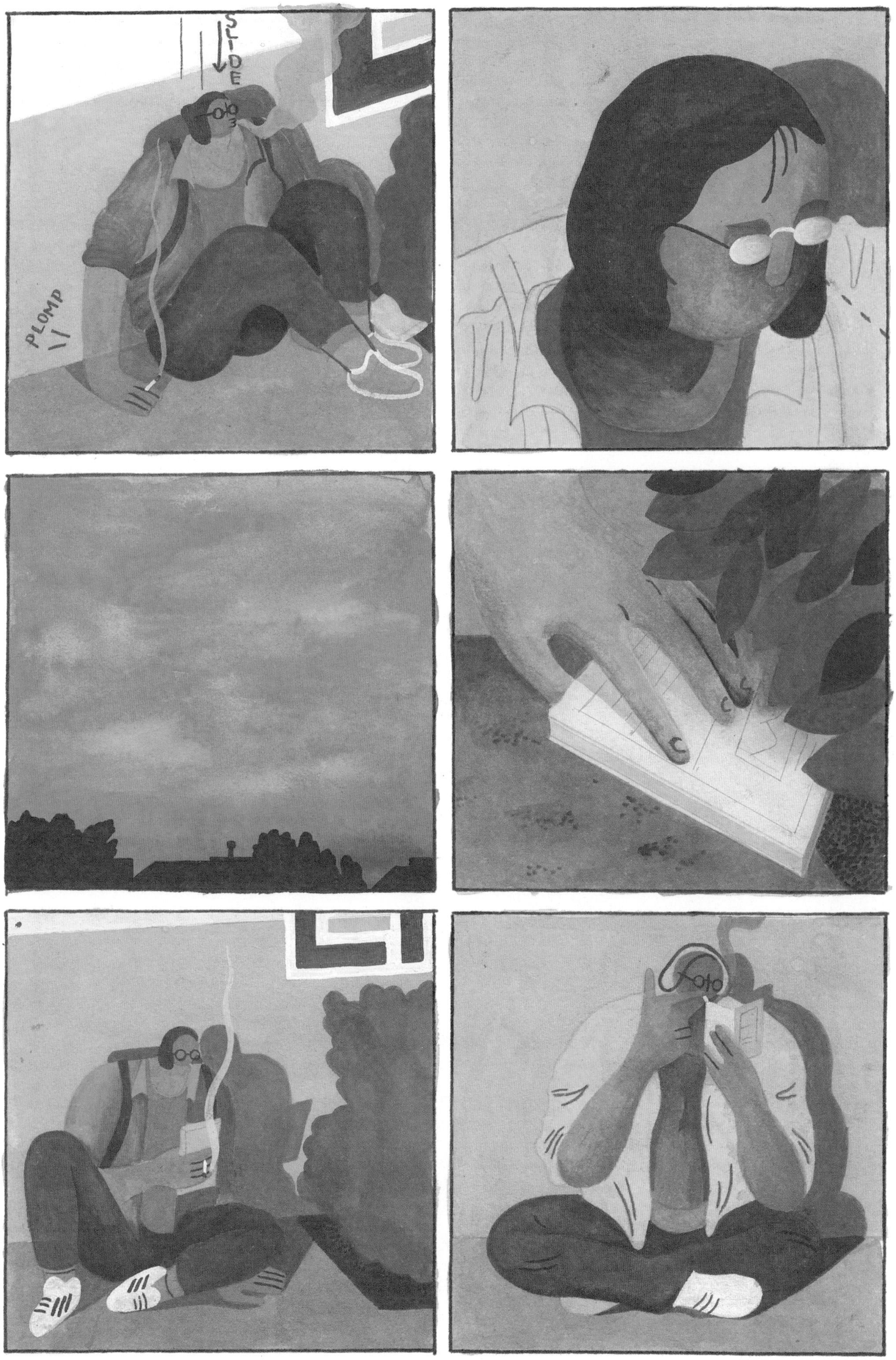
SLIDE
PLOMP

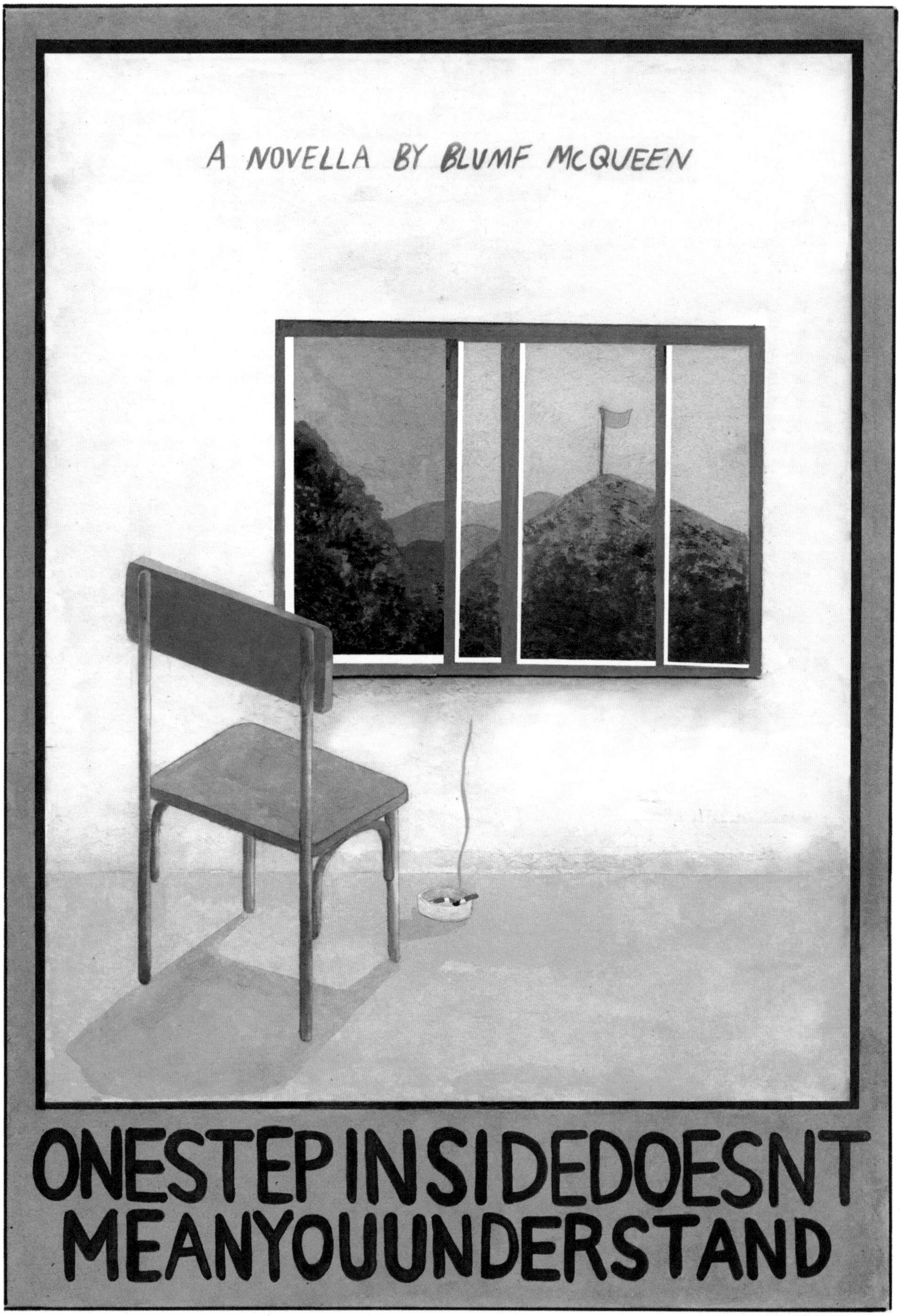
A NOVELLA BY BLUMF McQUEEN
ONESTEPINSIDEDOESNT
MEANYOUUNDERSTAND

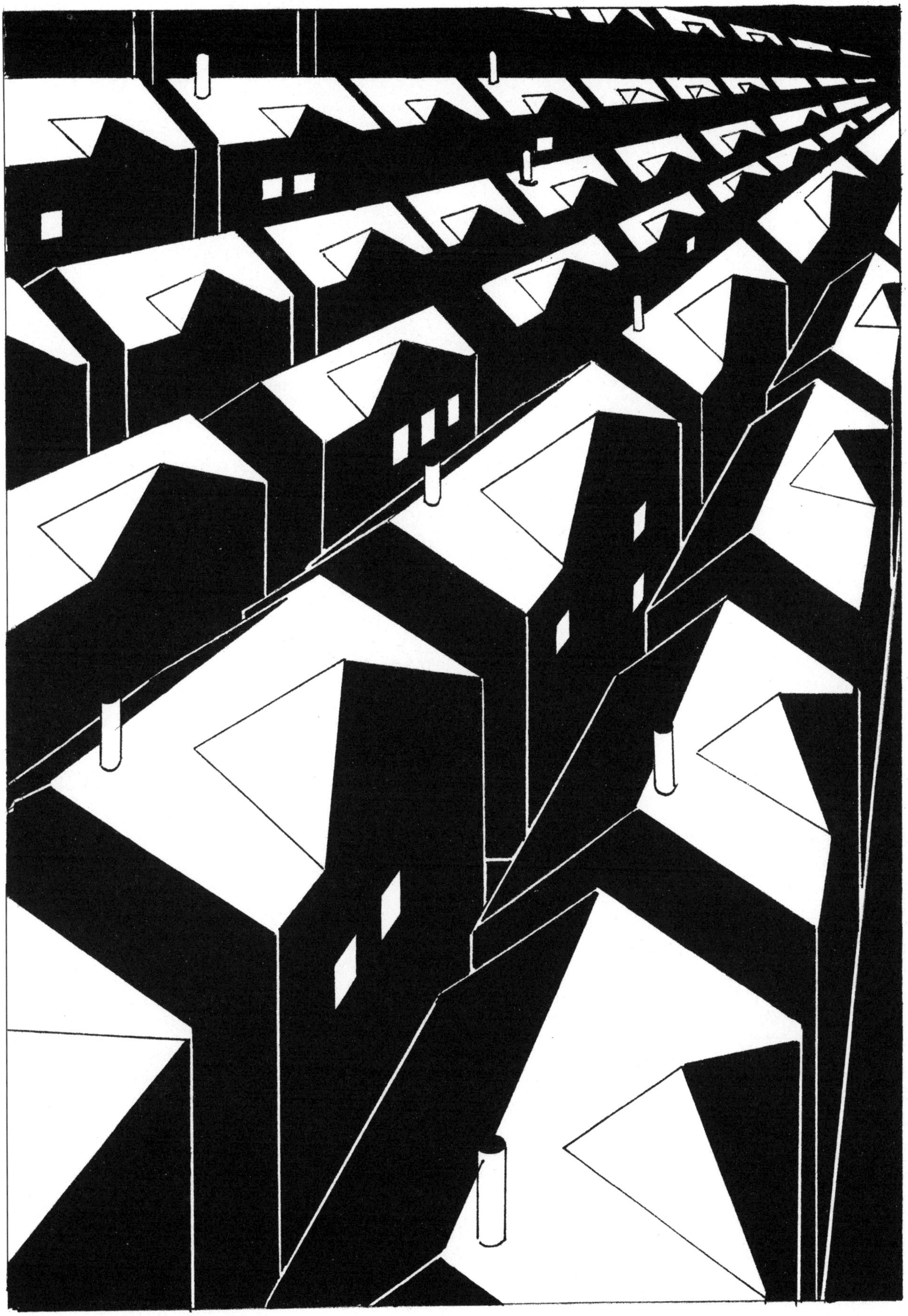

ONE STEP INSIDE DOESN'T
MEAN YOU UNDERSTAND

BLUMF McQUEEN

THIS BOOK IS DEDICATED TO PURE, UNCONDITIONAL, EVERLASTING LOVE.

'I WANT TO LIVE SOMEWHERE WITH A TIN ROOF'

HE'S WHISPERING TO ME WHILE WE LISTEN TO THE RAIN.

I'M TRANSFIXED, HE'S LIKE WATCHING A SLOW MOTION CAR CRASH. MUMBLING IN HIS SLEEP ABOUT HOW HE LOVES ME WITHOUT EVEN KNOWING MY NAME.

I LAUGH, BECAUSE THESE THINGS ARE ALWAYS FUNNY UNTIL THEY'RE NOT.

'I HATE THIS PLACE' HE TELLS ME ON THE FIRST NIGHT

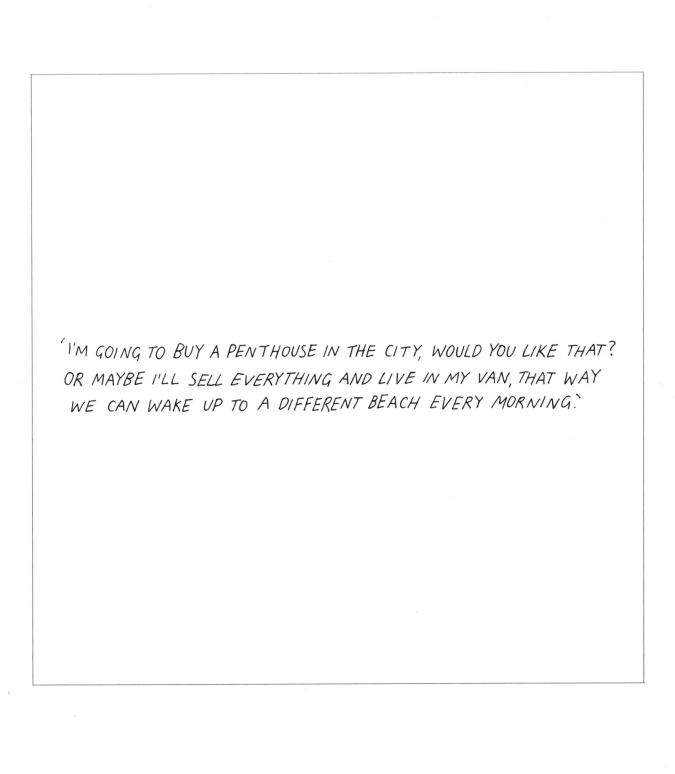

'I'M GOING TO BUY A PENTHOUSE IN THE CITY, WOULD YOU LIKE THAT?
OR MAYBE I'LL SELL EVERYTHING AND LIVE IN MY VAN, THAT WAY
WE CAN WAKE UP TO A DIFFERENT BEACH EVERY MORNING.'

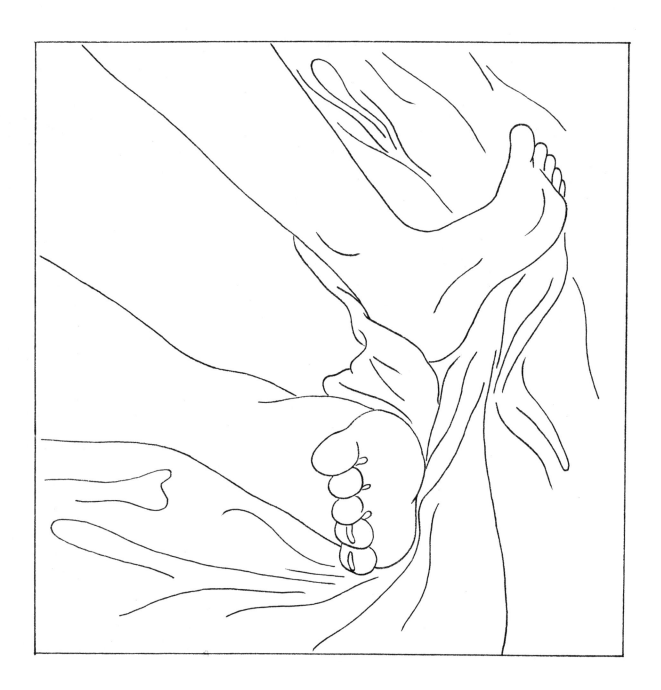

I SUDDENLY UNDERSTAND WHAT HE'S DOING, HE'S TRYING TO CONVINCE ME HE'S STILL ALIVE.

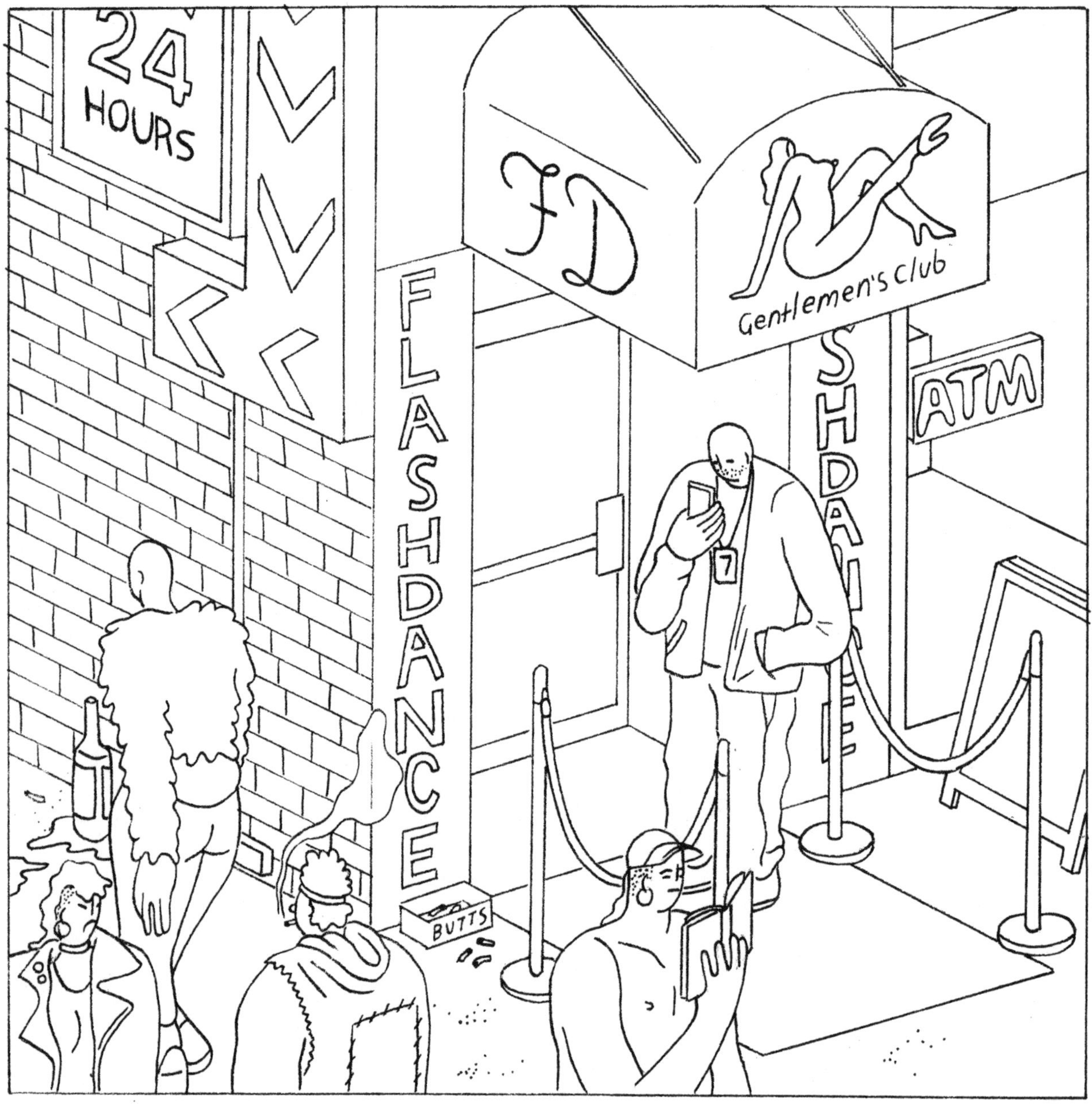
24
HOURS
FD
Gentlemen's club
FLASHDANCE
SHDANCE
ATM
BUTTS
7

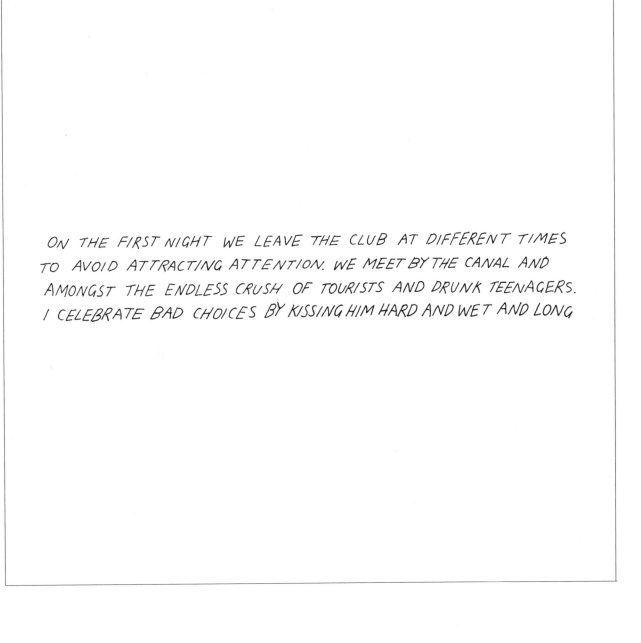

ON THE FIRST NIGHT WE LEAVE THE CLUB AT DIFFERENT TIMES
TO AVOID ATTRACTING ATTENTION. WE MEET BY THE CANAL AND
AMONGST THE ENDLESS CRUSH OF TOURISTS AND DRUNK TEENAGERS.
I CELEBRATE BAD CHOICES BY KISSING HIM HARD AND WET AND LONG

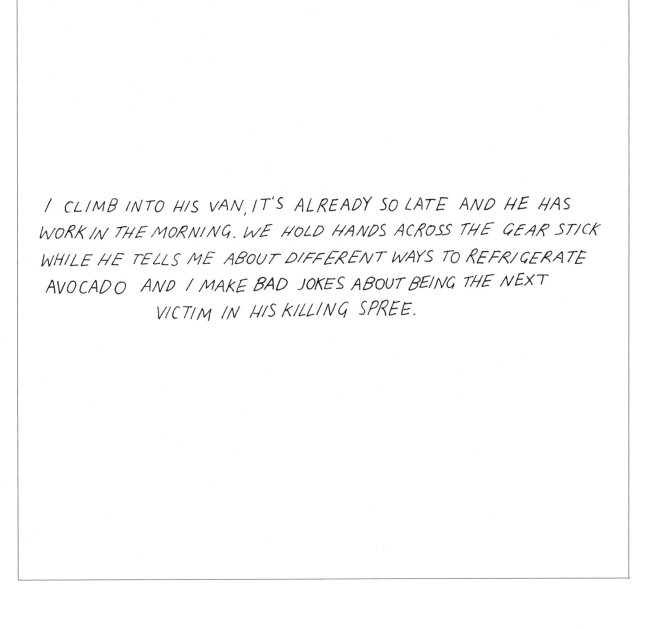

I CLIMB INTO HIS VAN, IT'S ALREADY SO LATE AND HE HAS WORK IN THE MORNING. WE HOLD HANDS ACROSS THE GEAR STICK WHILE HE TELLS ME ABOUT DIFFERENT WAYS TO REFRIGERATE AVOCADO AND I MAKE BAD JOKES ABOUT BEING THE NEXT VICTIM IN HIS KILLING SPREE.

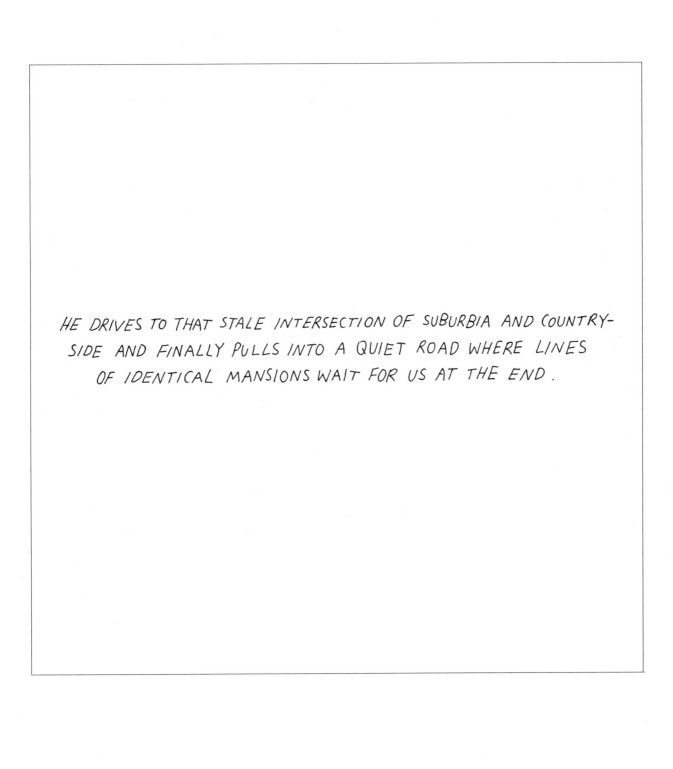

HE DRIVES TO THAT STALE INTERSECTION OF SUBURBIA AND COUNTRY-
SIDE AND FINALLY PULLS INTO A QUIET ROAD WHERE LINES
OF IDENTICAL MANSIONS WAIT FOR US AT THE END.

ON THE FIRST MORNING, THE SUN STILL DIPPED BELOW THE HORIZON, WE CLIMB INTO THE SHOWER TO CLEAN THE SEX OFF EACH OTHER'S BODIES. I SUDDENLY REALIZE I'M ARCHING MY BACK IN THE WAY TV HAS TAUGHT ME MEN LIKE. 'DON'T YOU DARE BREAK MY HEART' I WHISPER. GOD... WHO THE FUCK AM I?

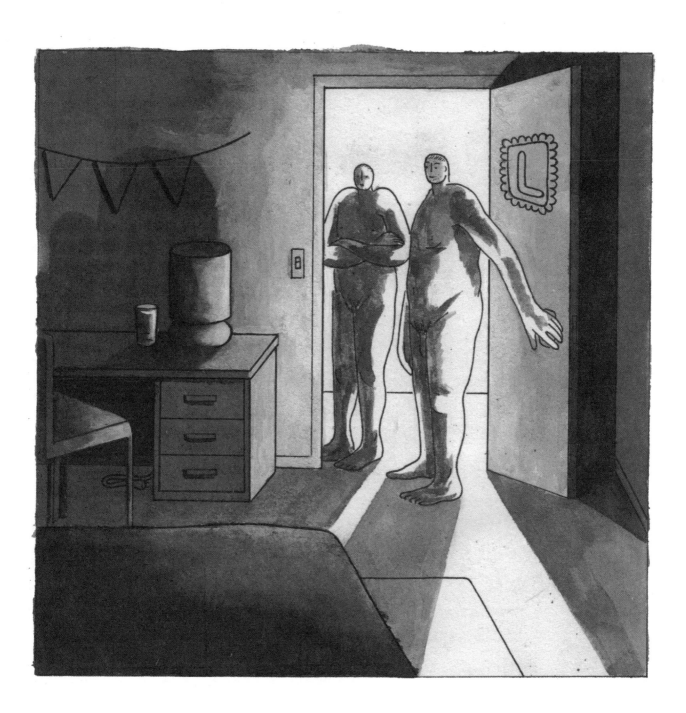

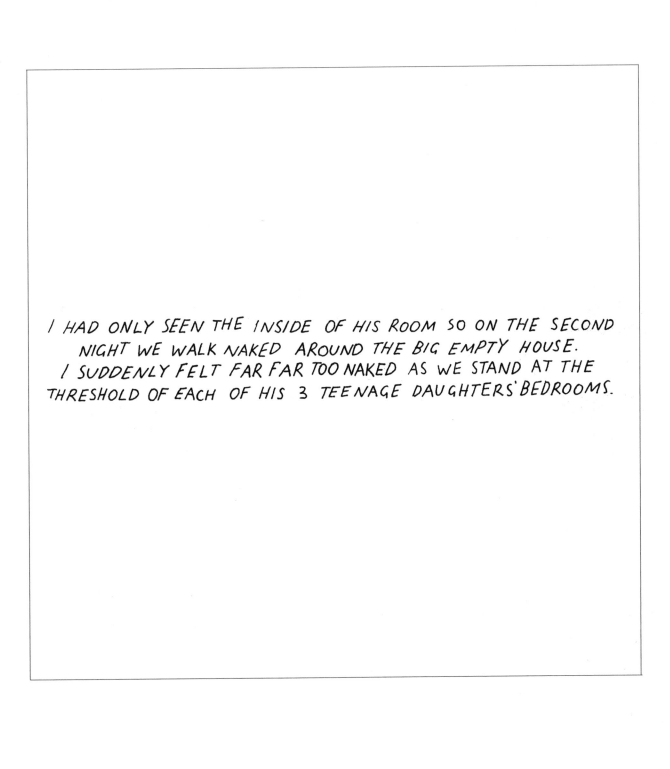

I HAD ONLY SEEN THE INSIDE OF HIS ROOM SO ON THE SECOND NIGHT WE WALK NAKED AROUND THE BIG EMPTY HOUSE.
I SUDDENLY FELT FAR FAR TOO NAKED AS WE STAND AT THE THRESHOLD OF EACH OF HIS 3 TEENAGE DAUGHTERS' BEDROOMS.

THE ROOMS REMIND ME OF SETS FROM AN IKEA CATALOGUE,
COLD SPACES LITTERED WITH AWKWARDLY HUNG PROPS ~
WEEKEND VISITATION RIGHTS ONLY.

I SHIFT MY WEIGHT UNCOMFORTABLY, THIS IS
BECOMING TOO FAMILIAR TO BE FUN.

WE MEET AT WORK. IT'S A SLOW NIGHT AND HE BUYS A $300 DANCE OFF ME, WE SIT AND TALK AND CUDDLE IN A DARK BOOTH AT THE BACK OF THE CLUB. HE TELLS ME ABOUT HIS KIDS AND TALKS ENDLESSLY ABOUT THE EX WHO JUST BROKE HIS HEART.

HE SAYS HIS SISTER WORKS BEHIND THE BAR AND INSISTS THAT HE'S ONLY HERE TO VISIT HER. HE TELLS ME HE KNOWS THIS PLACE ISN'T REAL.

I TAKE MY HEELS OFF SIPPING RED BULL AND CRANBERRY
WHILE OFFERING CRUMBS FROM MY LIFE. I TELL HIM THAT I'M
AN ARTIST AND THAT I DON'T REALLY SLEEP WITH MEN VERY
OFTEN.

I TAKE MY LONG BROWN WIG OFF AND SHOW HIM MY
SHAVED HEAD. THIS GESTURE OF SIMULATED VULNERABILITY
USUALLY GETS ME GOOD TIPS.

HE RUNS HIS INDEX FINGER ACROSS THE PATCHWORK OF SCARS DOWN MY INNER THIGH. I TELL HIM IT HELPS ME WHEN THERE'S NO AIR LEFT TO BREATHE.

HE HOLDS MY HAND AND LOOKS INTO MY EYES. 'WE CAN HELP EACH OTHER' HE SAYS, I CAN HELP HIM LEARN TO LIVE AGAIN AND HE CAN HELP ME BREATHE.

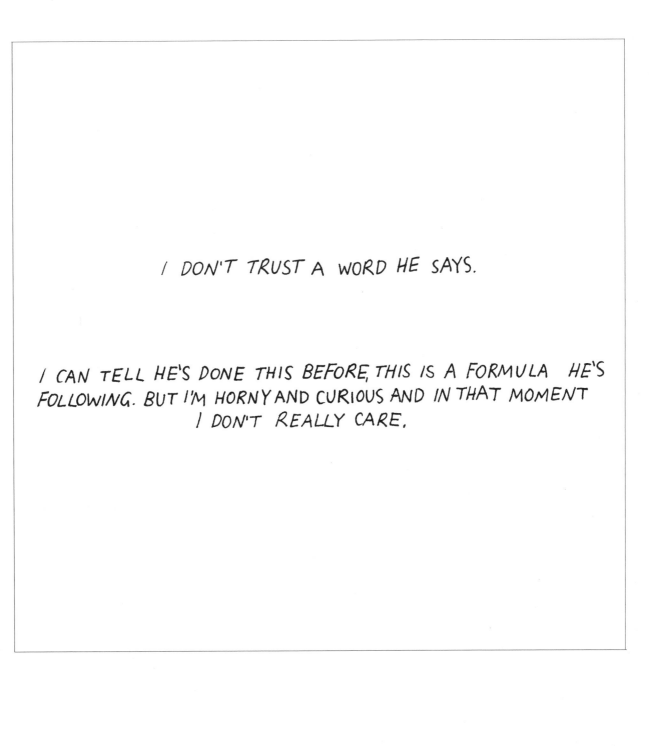

I DON'T TRUST A WORD HE SAYS.

I CAN TELL HE'S DONE THIS BEFORE, THIS IS A FORMULA HE'S FOLLOWING. BUT I'M HORNY AND CURIOUS AND IN THAT MOMENT I DON'T REALLY CARE.

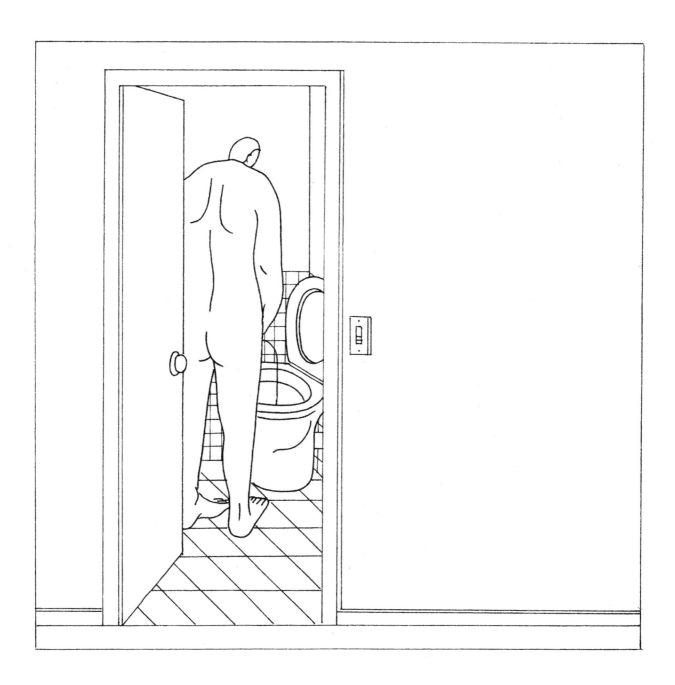

THE SEX WAS FUN BUT IN A FLEETING KIND OF WAY, MY GROWING
DISDAIN FOR HIM MUDDYING THE PLEASURE. HIS UNDERSTANDING OF
FUCKING WAS DISSAPOINTINGLY AND UNCREATIVELY HETEROSEXUAL.
THE WORLD BEGINNING AND ENDING WITH HIS COCK.

HOW CAN SOMEONE LEARN SO *LITTLE* IN ALL THOSE YEARS?

ON THE FINAL NIGHT HE TELLS ME ABOUT BEING RAISED BY A SINGLE MOTHER WHO WORKED A LOT, HE TELLS ME ABOUT STEALING COPPER PIPING WITH HIS COUSINS AS A TEEN AND LOSING HIS VIRGINITY AT 11.

DOWN THE HALL, IN THE SPACIOUS OPEN PLAN KITCHEN, THE MARBLE COUNTERTOPS OVERFLOW WITH DIRTY DISHES AND CANDY WRAPPERS. HE TALKS AND TALKS, I'M NOT LISTENING BUT HE DOESN'T SEEM TO NOTICE.

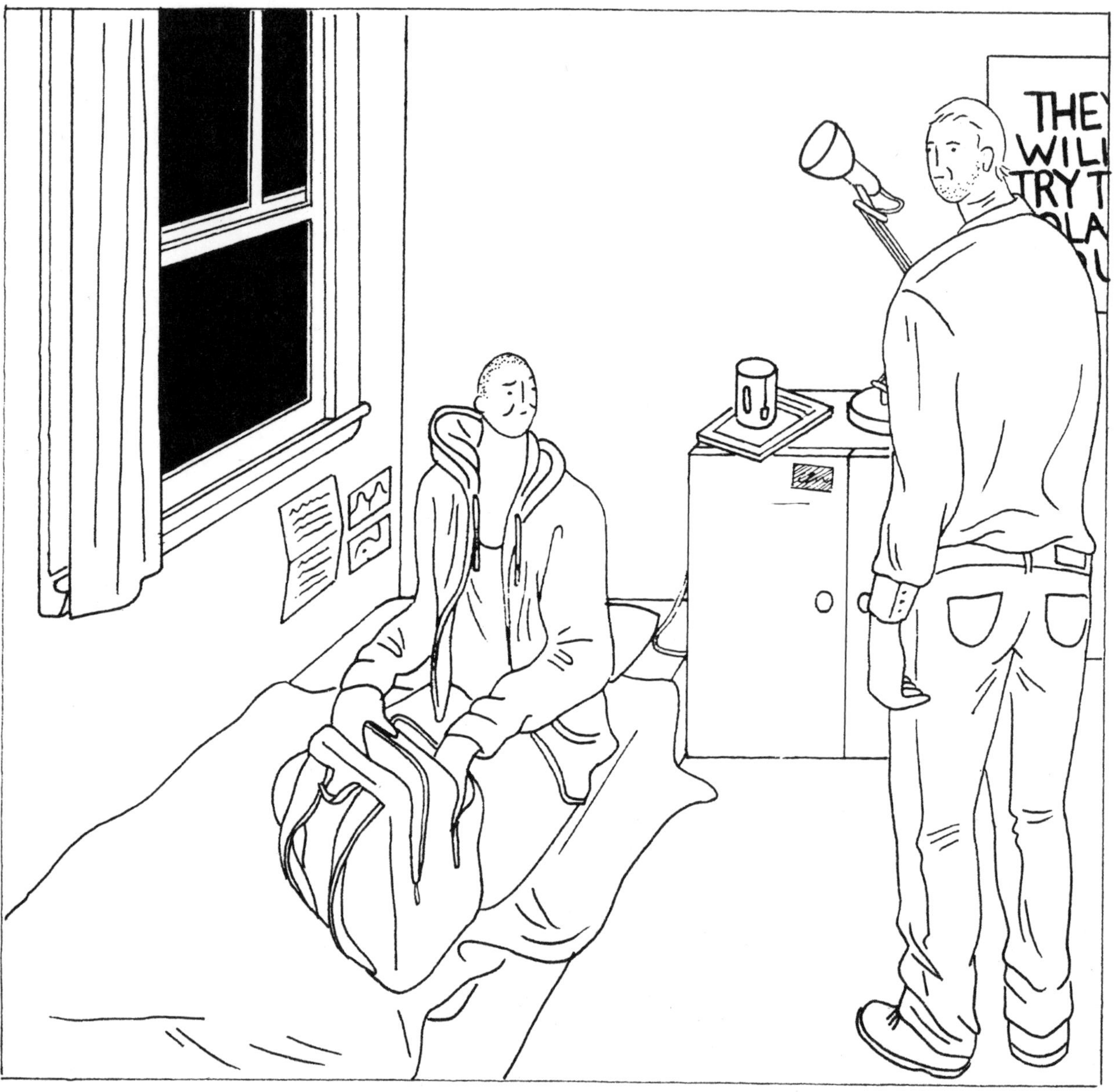
THEY
TRY

A FEW HOURS EARLIER HE PICKS ME UP FOR DINNER.
I WATCH AS HE STANDS STIFFLY IN THE CENTER OF THE
BEDROOM WHILE I GET MY THINGS.

'DON'T BE EMBARRASSED' HE TELLS ME AFTER A PROLONGED
SILENCE, AND FOR A LONG MOMENT I DON'T UNDERSTAND
WHAT HE COULD MEAN.

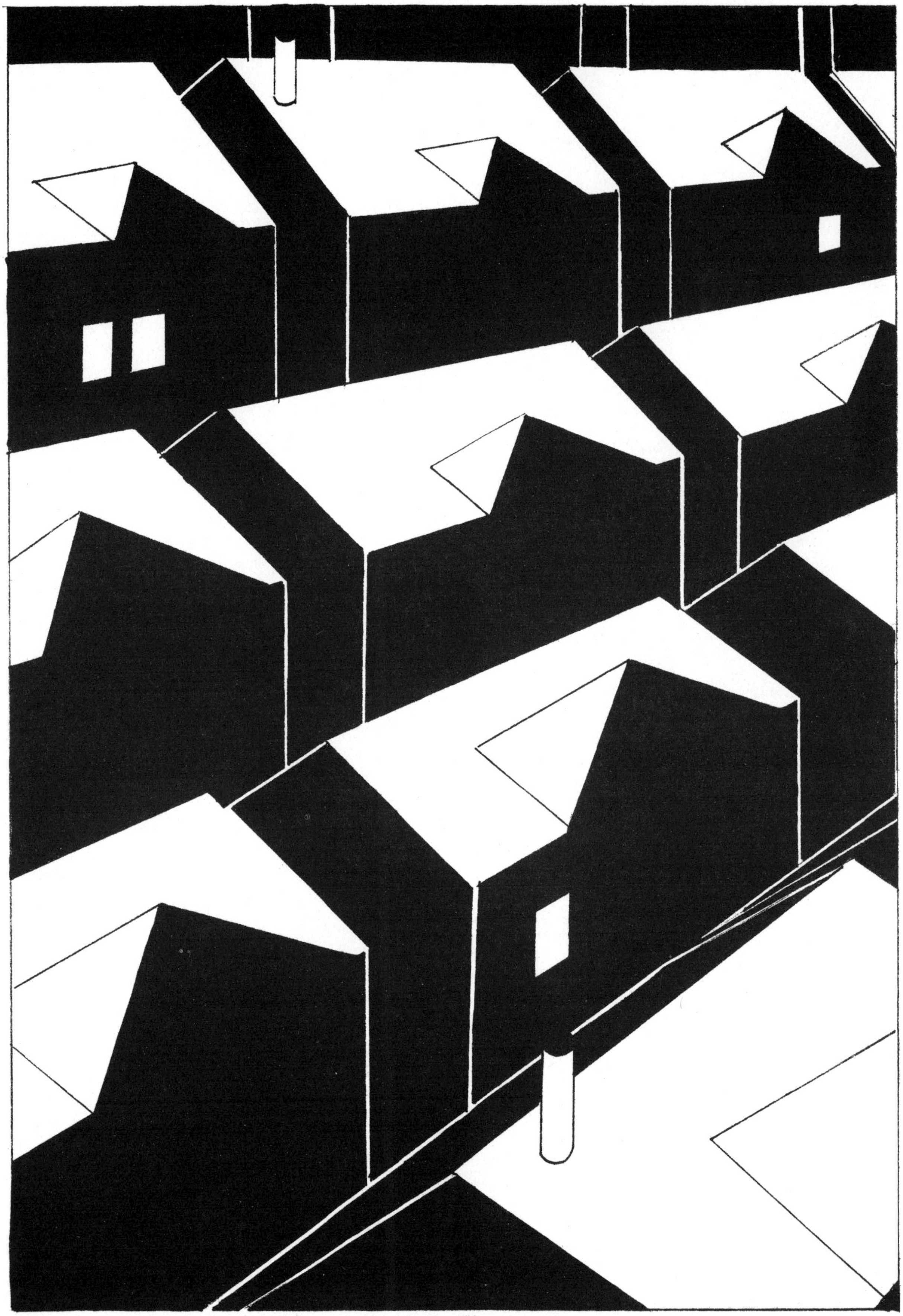

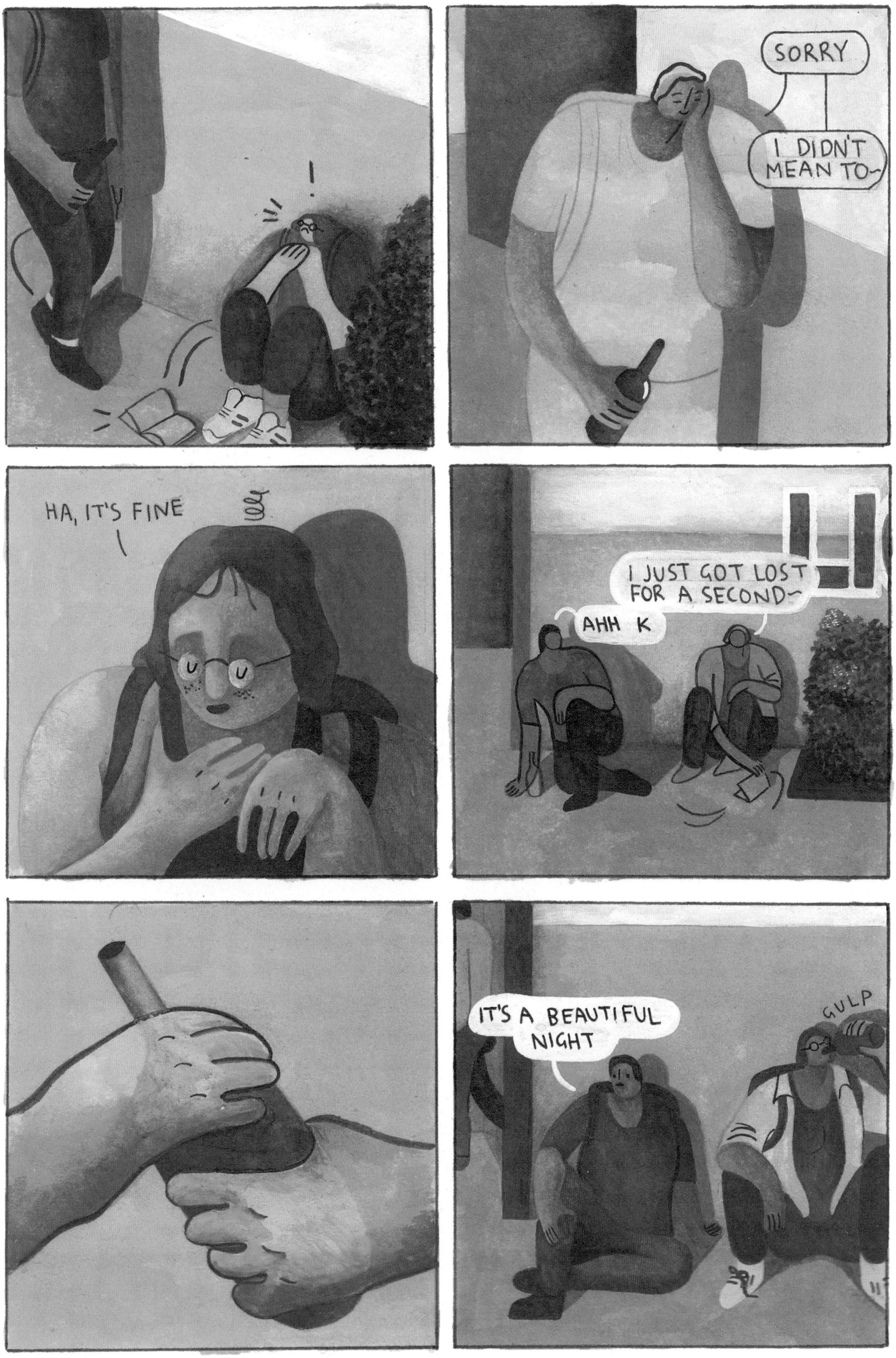
!
SORRY
I DIDN'T MEAN TO~
HA, IT'S FINE
I JUST GOT LOST FOR A SECOND~
AHH K
IT'S A BEAUTIFUL NIGHT
GULP

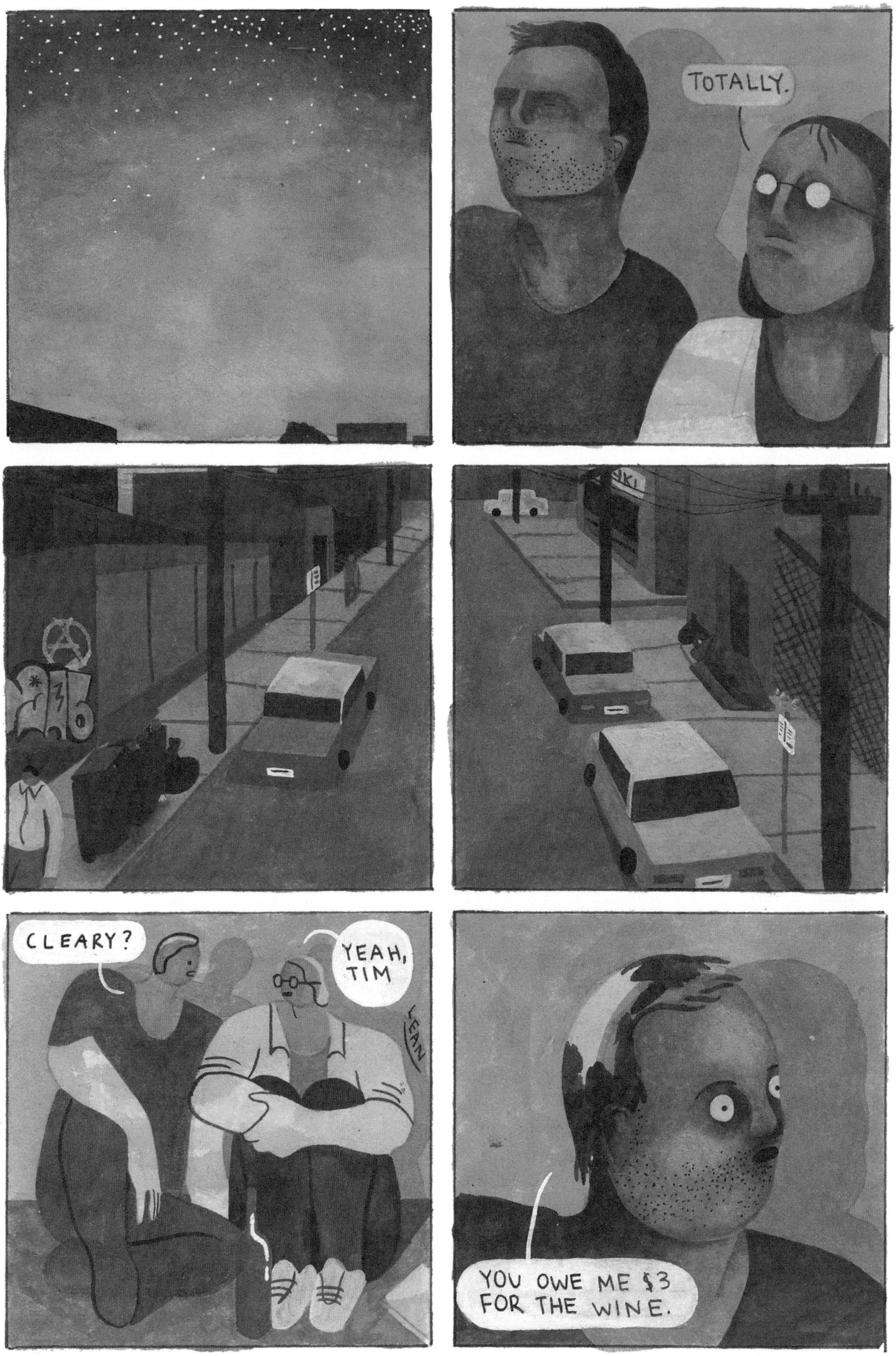
TOTALLY.
CLEARY?
YEAH, TIM
LEAN
YOU OWE ME $3 FOR THE WINE.

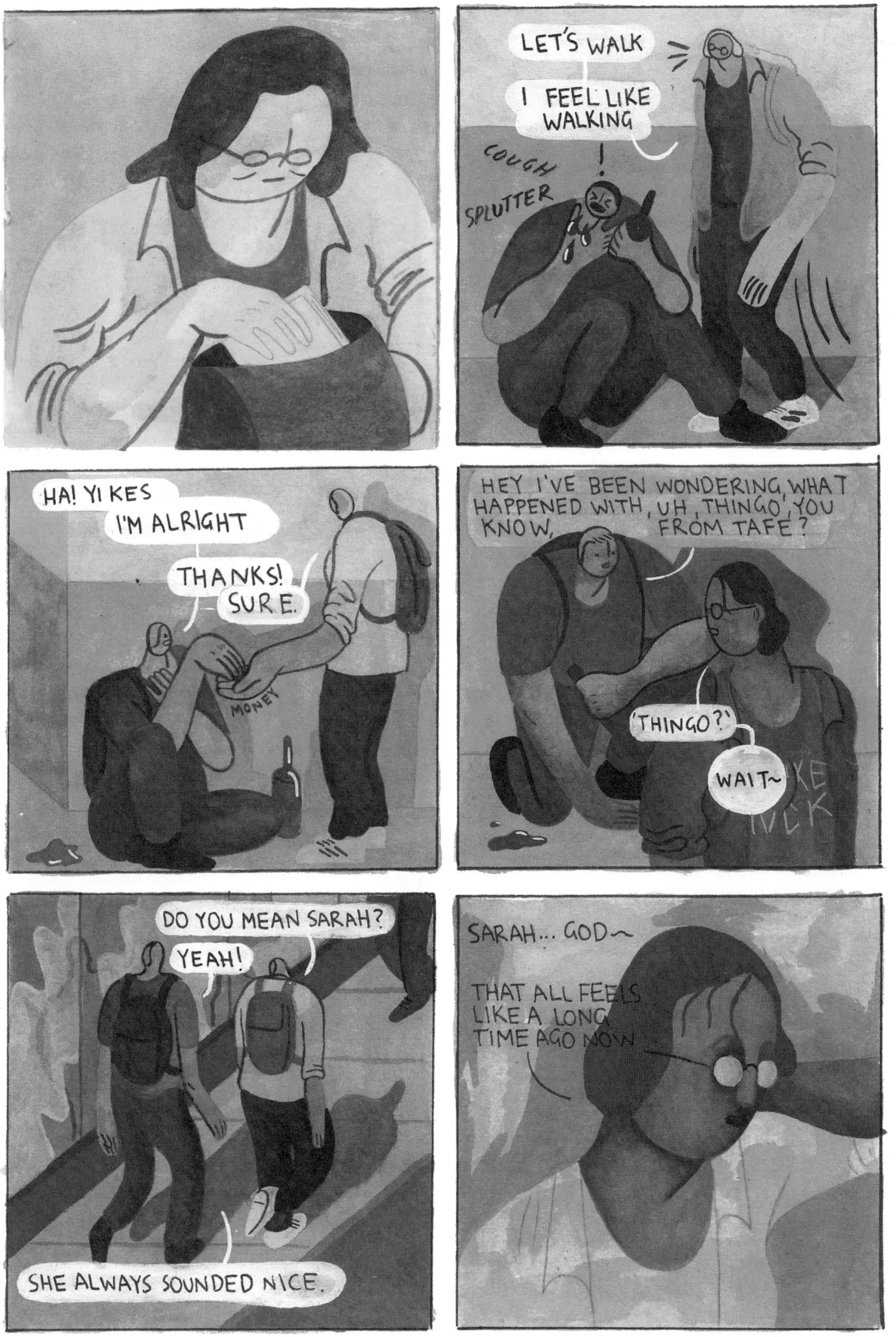
LET'S WALK
I FEEL LIKE WALKING
COUGH
SPLUTTER
HA! YIKES
I'M ALRIGHT
THANKS!
SURE.
MONEY
HEY I'VE BEEN WONDERING, WHAT HAPPENED WITH, UH, 'THINGO', YOU KNOW, FROM TAFE?
'THINGO?'
WAIT~
DO YOU MEAN SARAH?
YEAH!
SHE ALWAYS SOUNDED NICE.
SARAH... GOD~
THAT ALL FEELS LIKE A LONG TIME AGO NOW

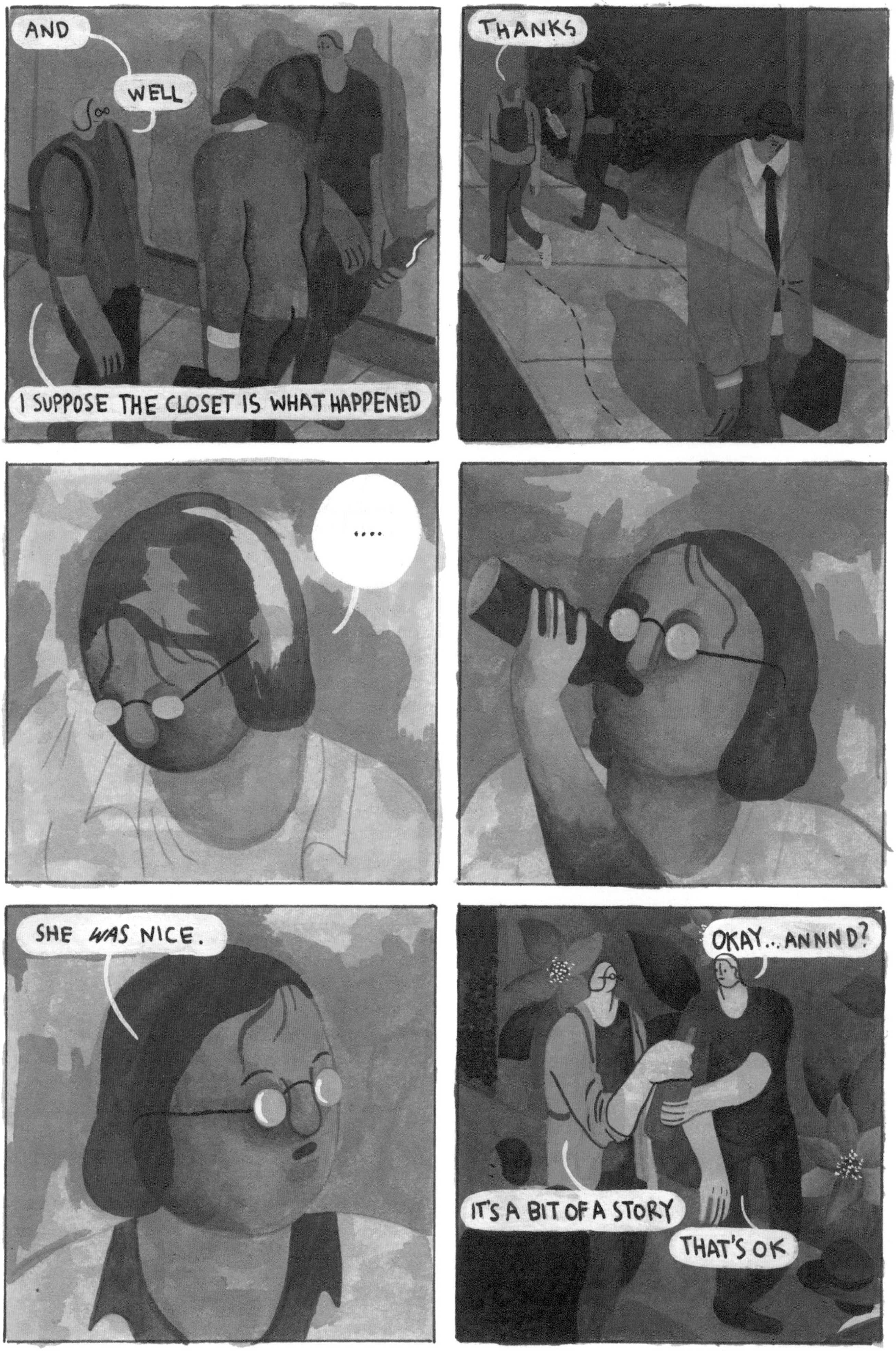
AND
WELL
I SUPPOSE THE CLOSET IS WHAT HAPPENED
THANKS
....
SHE WAS NICE.
OKAY... ANNND?
IT'S A BIT OF A STORY
THAT'S OK

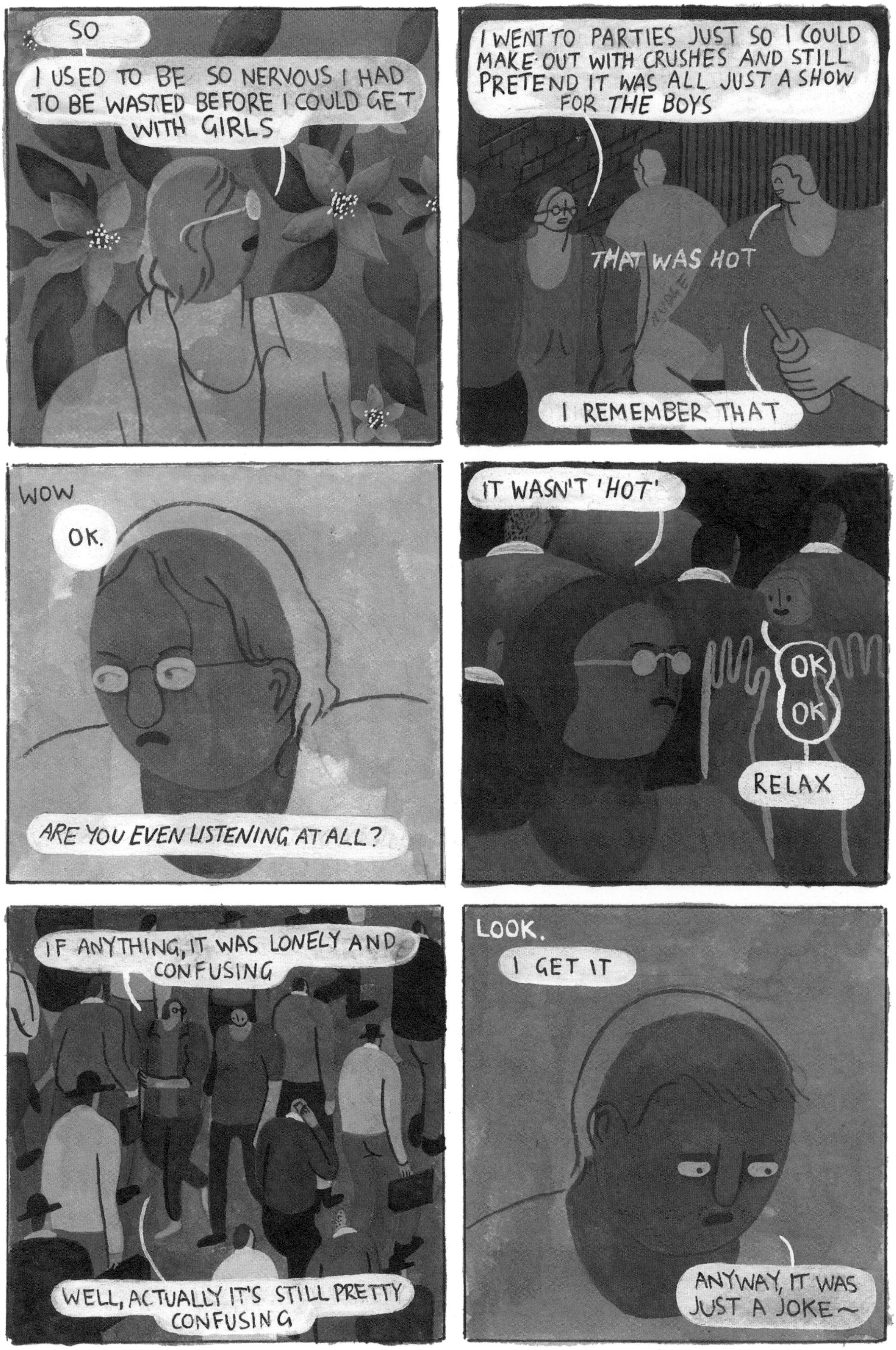
SO
I USED TO BE SO NERVOUS I HAD TO BE WASTED BEFORE I COULD GET WITH GIRLS
I WENT TO PARTIES JUST SO I COULD MAKE OUT WITH CRUSHES AND STILL PRETEND IT WAS ALL JUST A SHOW FOR THE BOYS
THAT WAS HOT
I REMEMBER THAT
WOW
OK.
ARE YOU EVEN LISTENING AT ALL?
IT WASN'T 'HOT'
OK
OK
RELAX
IF ANYTHING, IT WAS LONELY AND CONFUSING
WELL, ACTUALLY IT'S STILL PRETTY CONFUSING
LOOK.
I GET IT
ANYWAY, IT WAS JUST A JOKE~

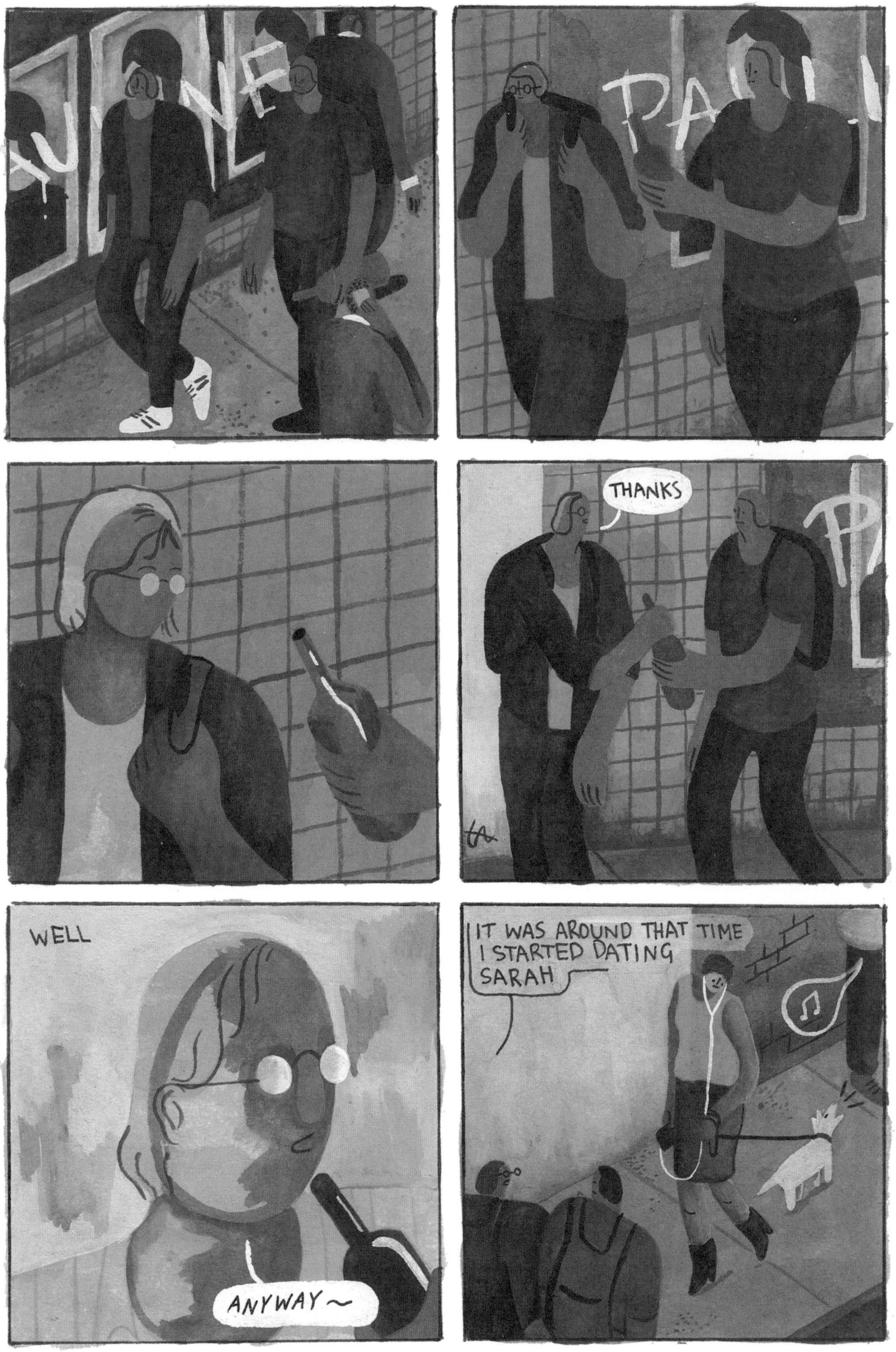
THANKS
WELL
ANYWAY~
IT WAS AROUND THAT TIME I STARTED DATING SARAH

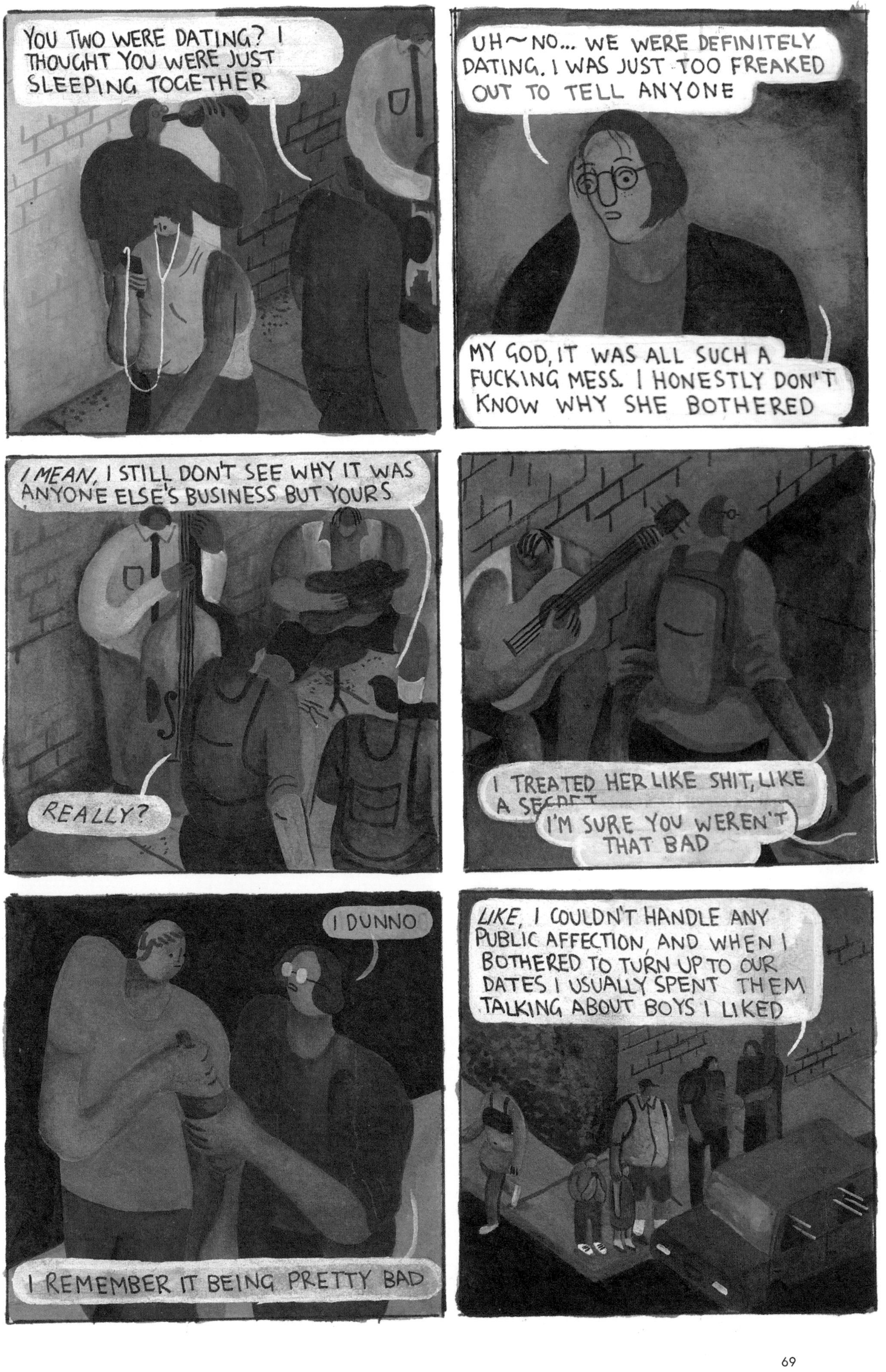
YOU TWO WERE DATING? I THOUGHT YOU WERE JUST SLEEPING TOGETHER
UH~NO... WE WERE DEFINITELY DATING. I WAS JUST TOO FREAKED OUT TO TELL ANYONE
MY GOD, IT WAS ALL SUCH A FUCKING MESS. I HONESTLY DON'T KNOW WHY SHE BOTHERED
I MEAN, I STILL DON'T SEE WHY IT WAS ANYONE ELSE'S BUSINESS BUT YOURS
REALLY?
I TREATED HER LIKE SHIT, LIKE A SE
I'M SURE YOU WEREN'T THAT BAD
I DUNNO
I REMEMBER IT BEING PRETTY BAD
LIKE, I COULDN'T HANDLE ANY PUBLIC AFFECTION, AND WHEN I BOTHERED TO TURN UP TO OUR DATES I USUALLY SPENT THEM TALKING ABOUT BOYS I LIKED

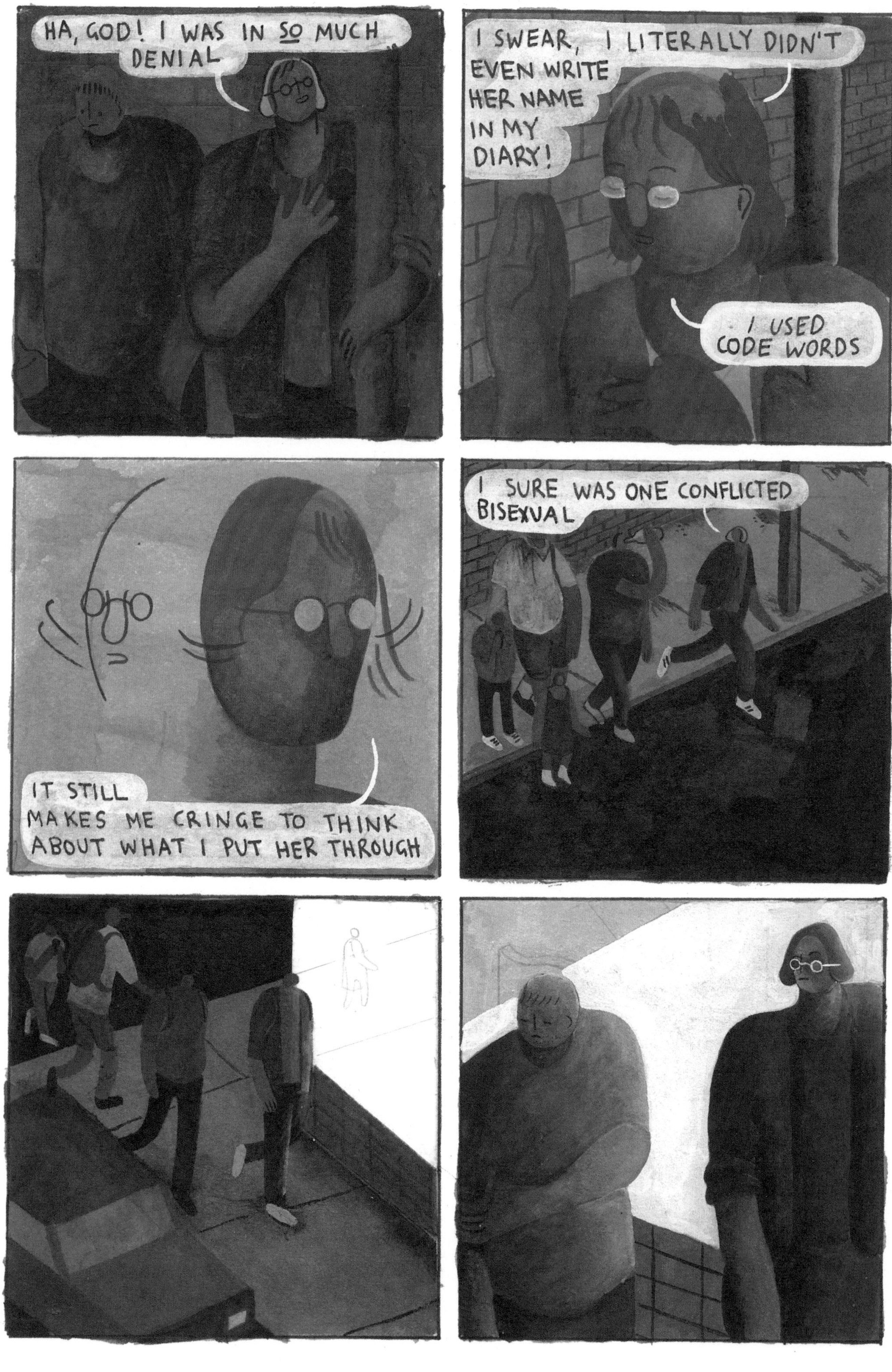
HA, GOD! I WAS IN SO MUCH DENIAL
I SWEAR, I LITERALLY DIDN'T EVEN WRITE HER NAME IN MY DIARY!
I USED CODE WORDS
IT STILL MAKES ME CRINGE TO THINK ABOUT WHAT I PUT HER THROUGH
I SURE WAS ONE CONFLICTED BISEXUAL

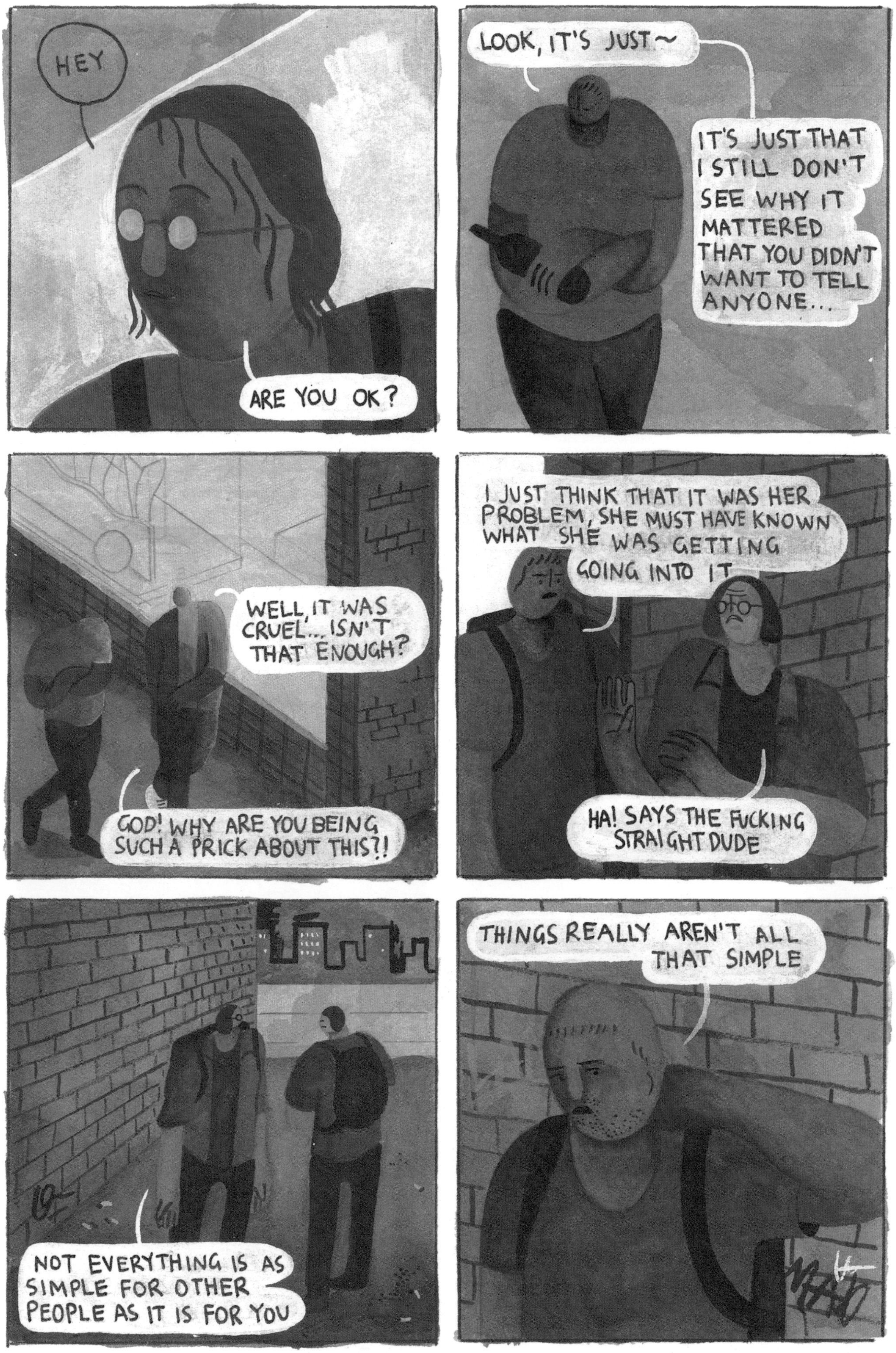
HEY
ARE YOU OK?
LOOK, IT'S JUST~
IT'S JUST THAT I STILL DON'T SEE WHY IT MATTERED THAT YOU DIDN'T WANT TO TELL ANYONE...
WELL, IT WAS CRUEL... ISN'T THAT ENOUGH?
GOD! WHY ARE YOU BEING SUCH A PRICK ABOUT THIS?!
I JUST THINK THAT IT WAS HER PROBLEM, SHE MUST HAVE KNOWN WHAT SHE WAS GETTING GOING INTO IT
HA! SAYS THE FUCKING STRAIGHT DUDE
NOT EVERYTHING IS AS SIMPLE FOR OTHER PEOPLE AS IT IS FOR YOU
THINGS REALLY AREN'T ALL THAT SIMPLE

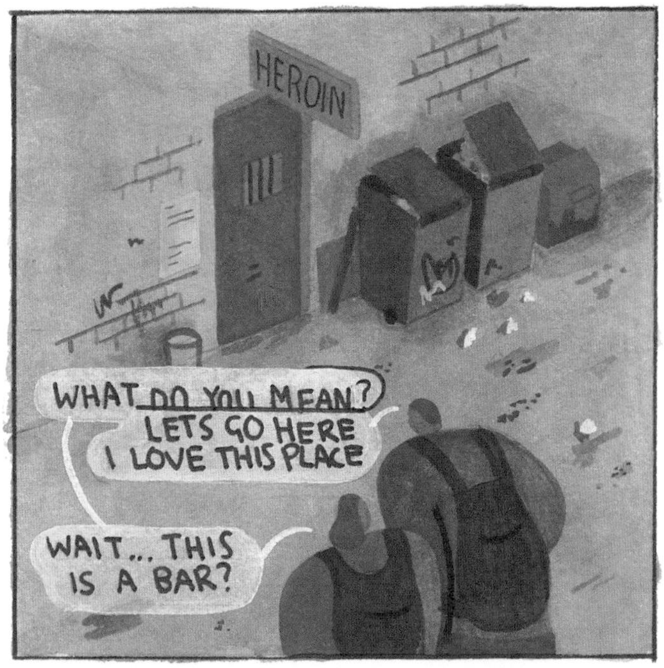
HEROIN
WHAT DO YOU MEAN?
LETS GO HERE I LOVE THIS PLACE
WAIT... THIS IS A BAR?
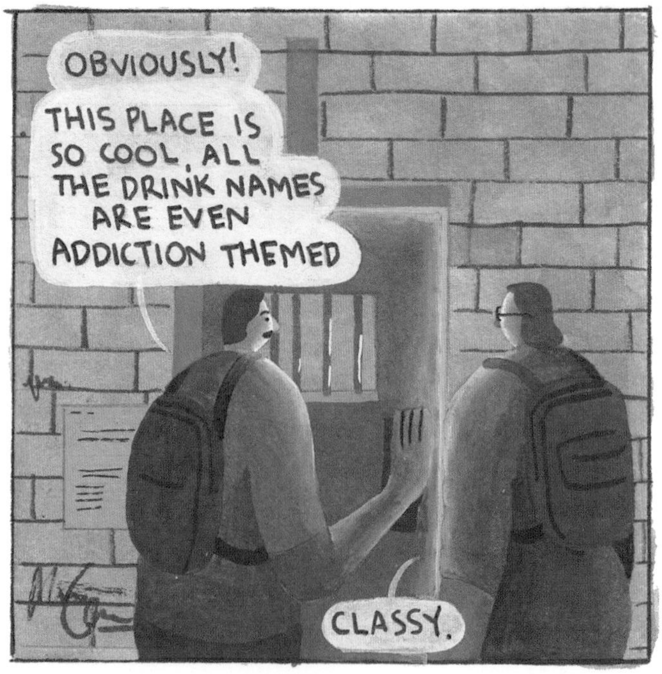
OBVIOUSLY!
THIS PLACE IS SO COOL, ALL THE DRINK NAMES ARE EVEN ADDICTION THEMED
CLASSY.
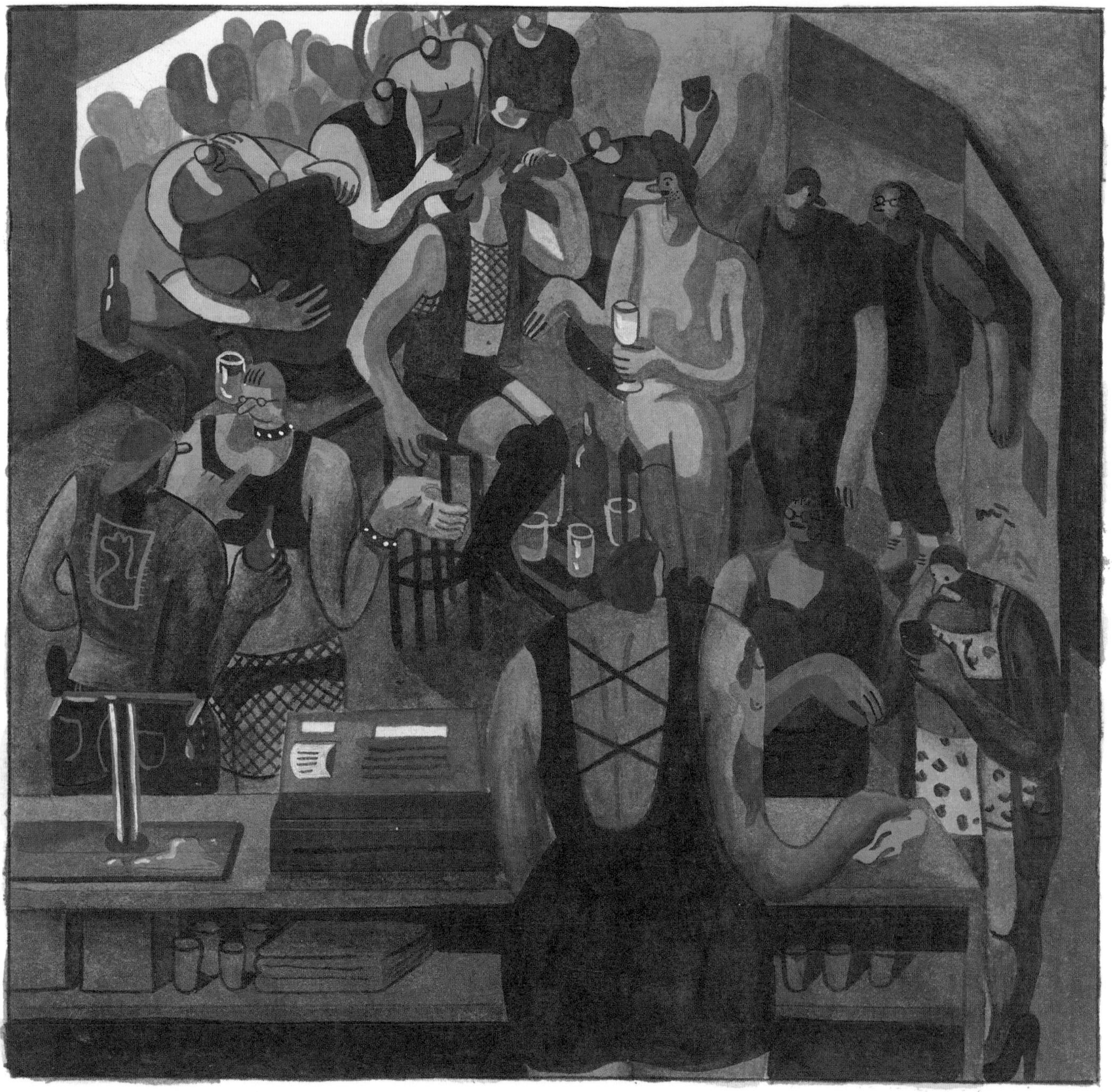

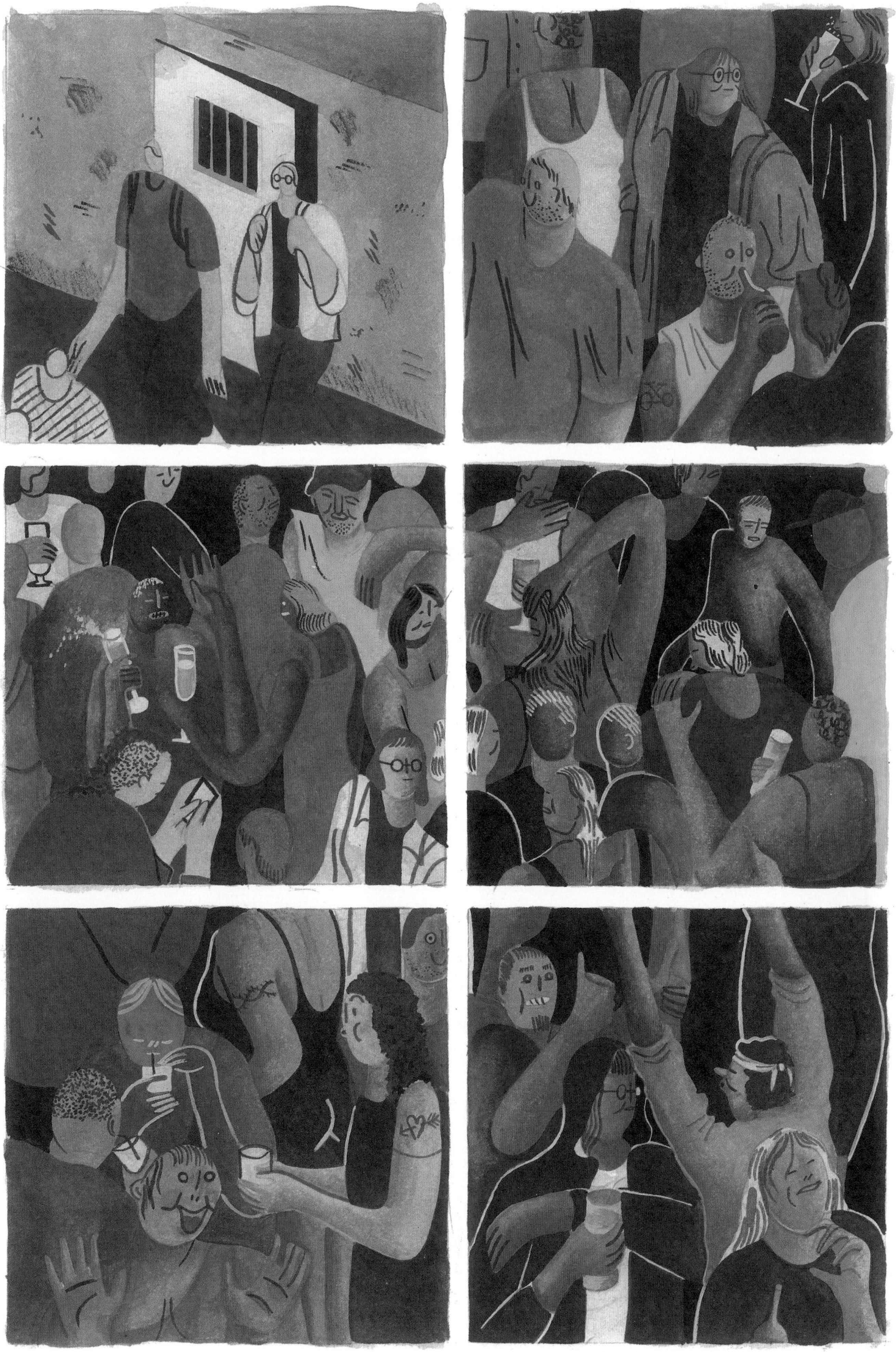

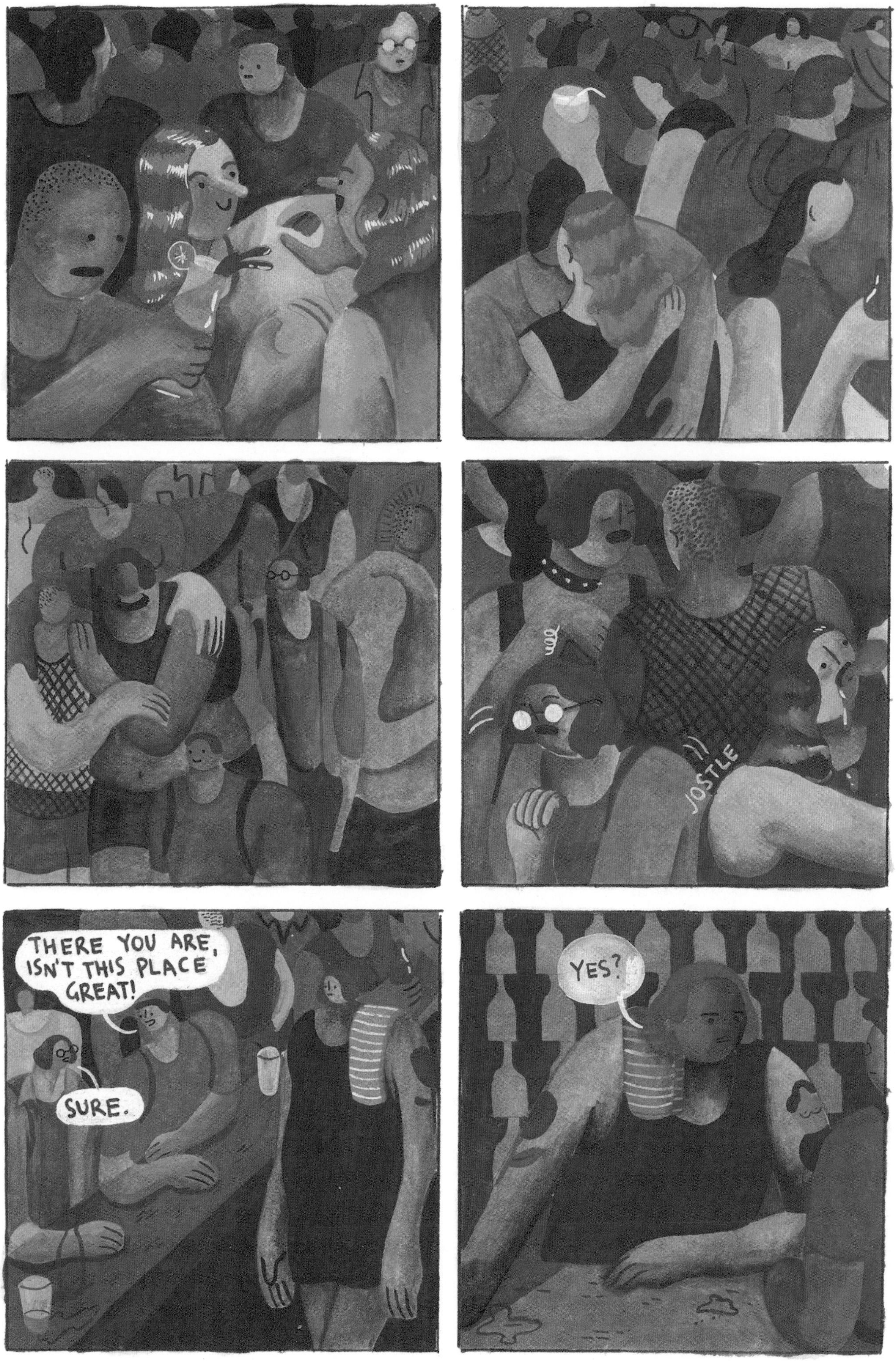
JOSTLE
THERE YOU ARE, ISN'T THIS PLACE GREAT!
SURE.
YES?

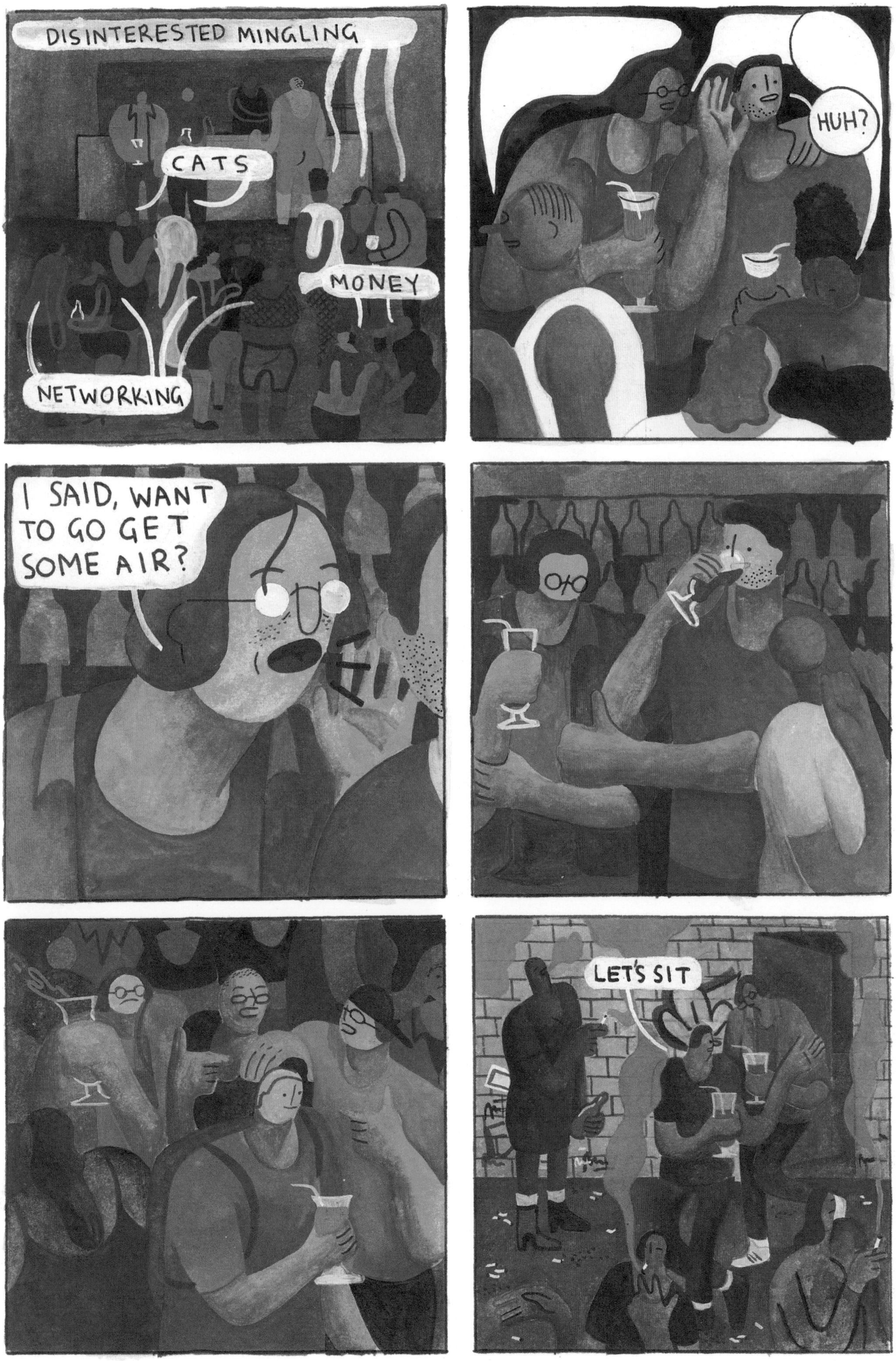
DISINTERESTED MINGLING
CATS
MONEY
NETWORKING
HUH?
I SAID, WANT TO GO GET SOME AIR?
LET'S SIT

SO ANYWAY
CONSIDERING HOW CLOSE WE WERE
AND WELL
HOW MESSY THAT WHOLE PERIOD WAS
DID YOU EVER THINK IT WAS WEIRD THAT WE NEVER HOOKED UP?
HAHA HAHA HAHA HAHA
DON'T BE DISGUSTING!

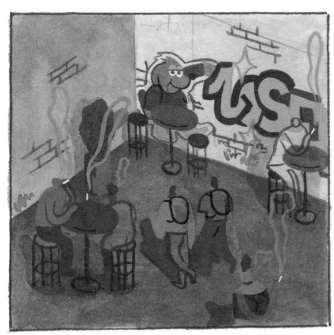

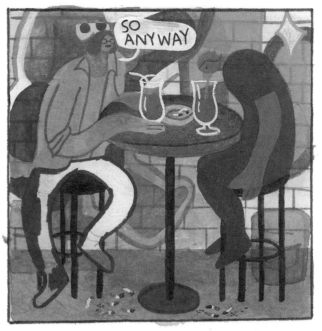

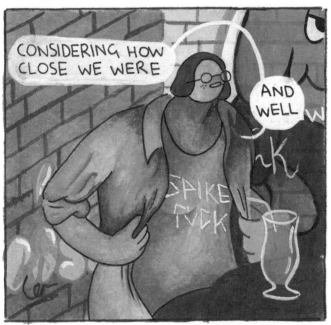

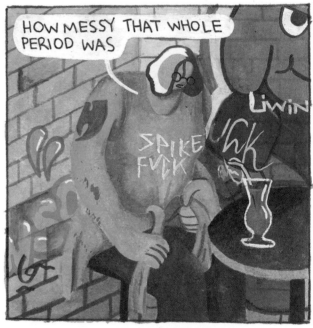

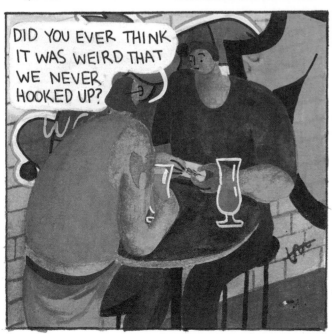

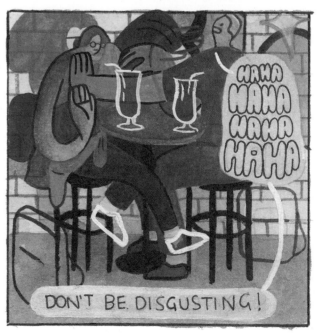

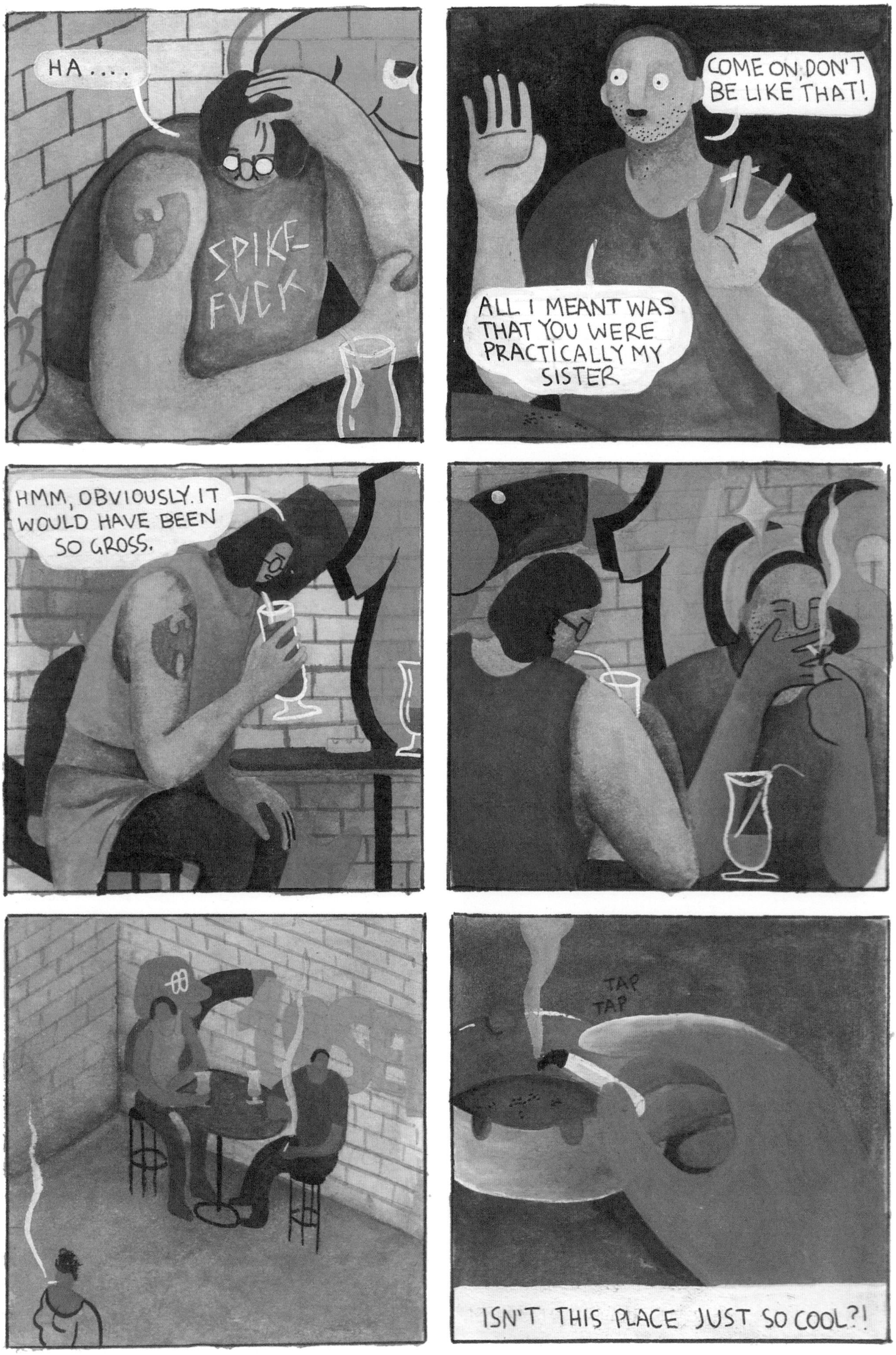
HA.....
SPIKE FVCK
COME ON, DON'T BE LIKE THAT!
ALL I MEANT WAS THAT YOU WERE PRACTICALLY MY SISTER
HMM, OBVIOUSLY. IT WOULD HAVE BEEN SO GROSS.
TAP TAP
ISN'T THIS PLACE JUST SO COOL?!

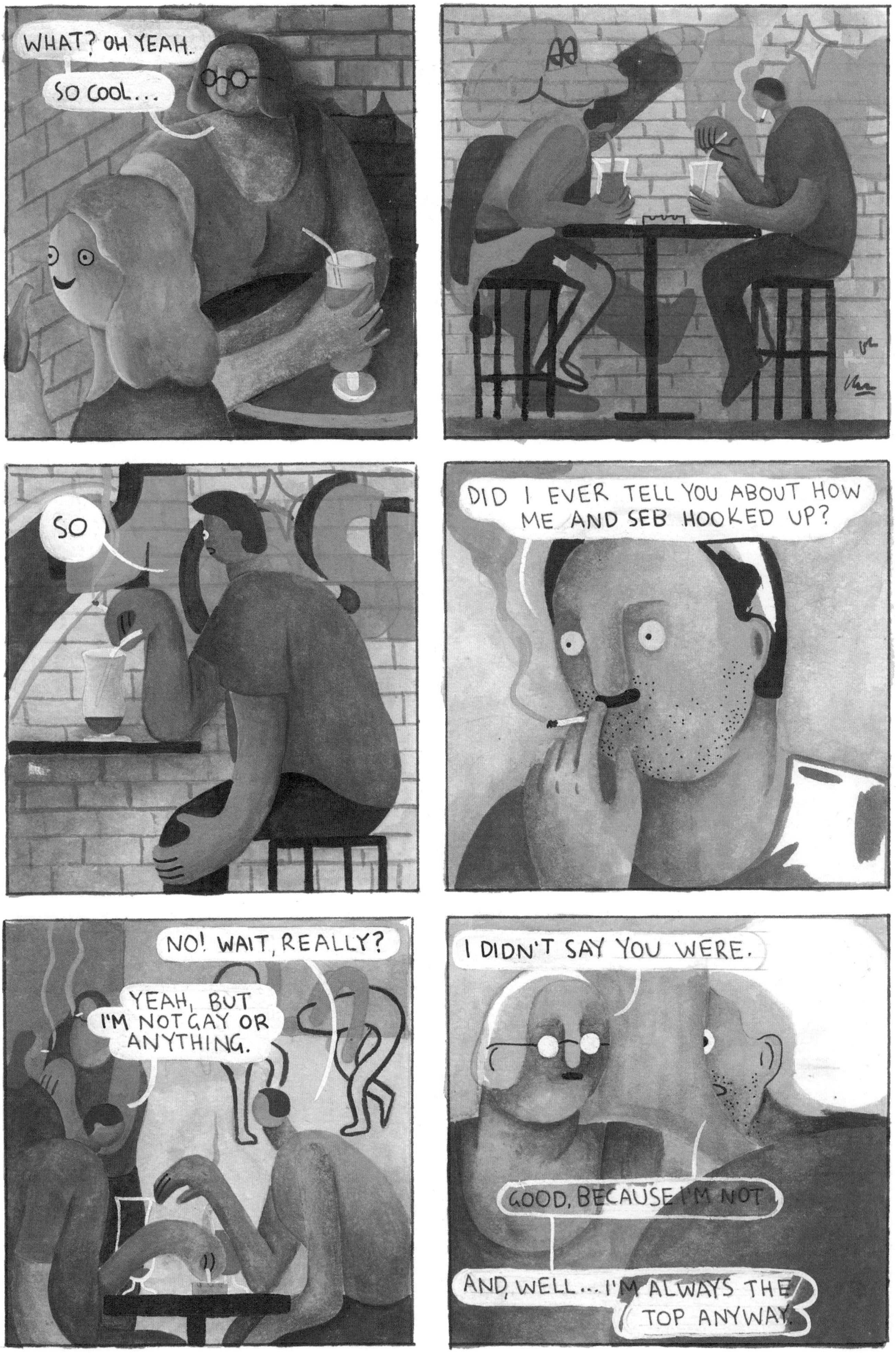
WHAT? OH YEAH..
SO COOL...
SO
DID I EVER TELL YOU ABOUT HOW ME AND SEB HOOKED UP?
NO! WAIT, REALLY?
YEAH, BUT I'M NOT GAY OR ANYTHING.
I DIDN'T SAY YOU WERE.
GOOD, BECAUSE I'M NOT
AND, WELL... I'M ALWAYS THE TOP ANYWAY.

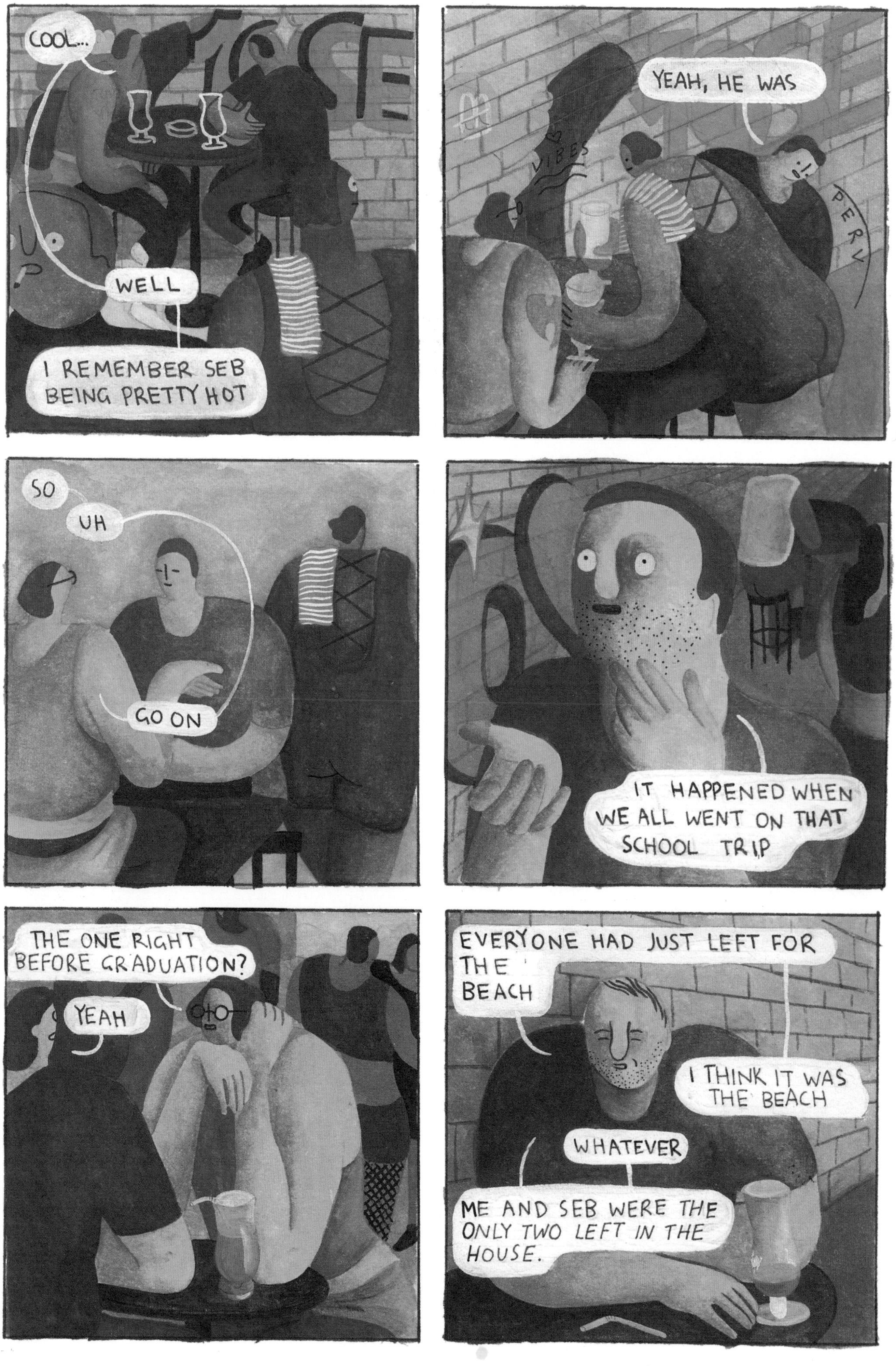
COOL...
WELL
I REMEMBER SEB BEING PRETTY HOT
YEAH, HE WAS
VIBES
PERV
SO
UH
GO ON
IT HAPPENED WHEN WE ALL WENT ON THAT SCHOOL TRIP
THE ONE RIGHT BEFORE GRADUATION?
YEAH
EVERYONE HAD JUST LEFT FOR THE BEACH
I THINK IT WAS THE BEACH
WHATEVER
ME AND SEB WERE THE ONLY TWO LEFT IN THE HOUSE.

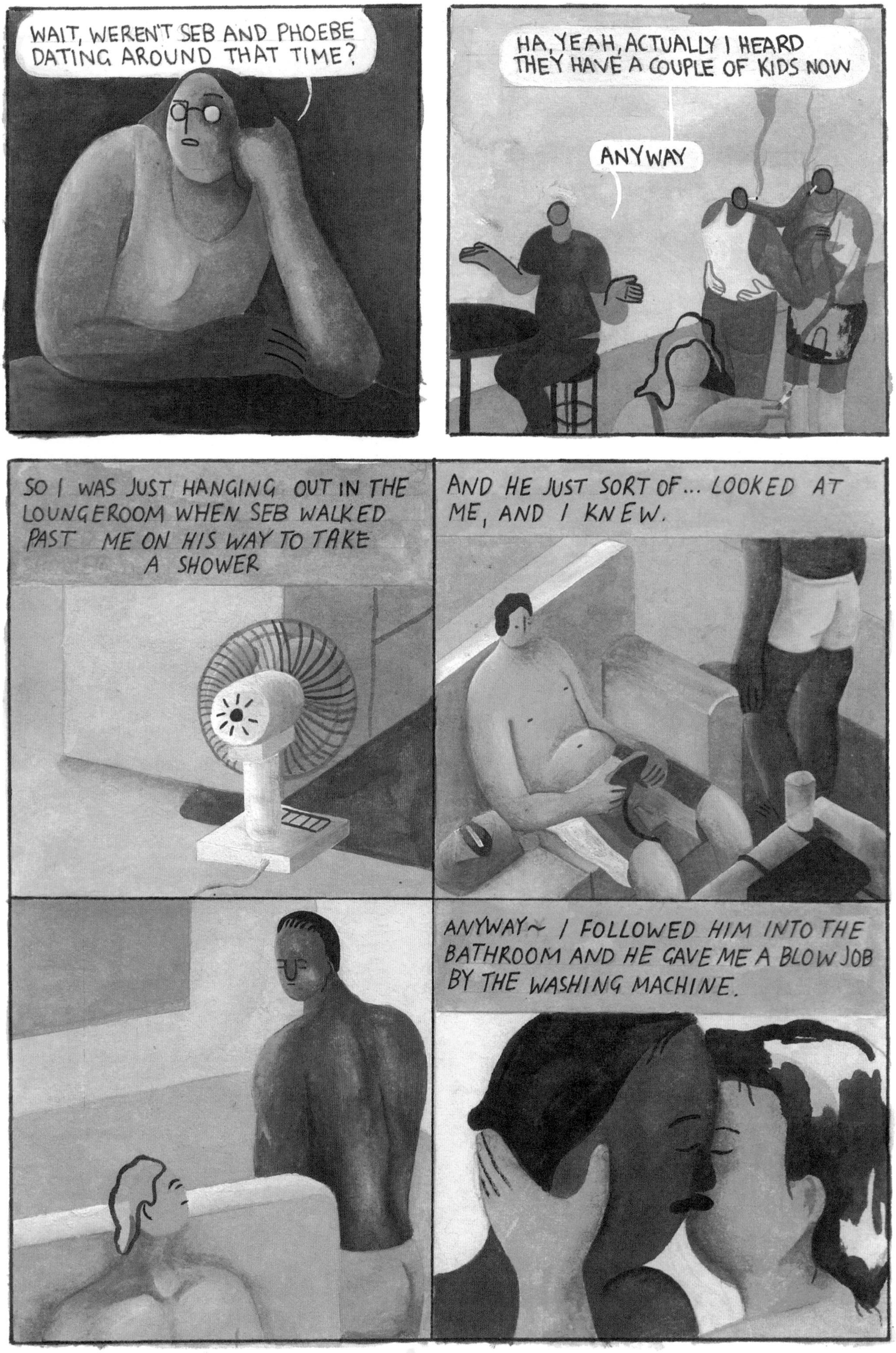
WAIT, WEREN'T SEB AND PHOEBE DATING AROUND THAT TIME?
HA, YEAH, ACTUALLY I HEARD THEY HAVE A COUPLE OF KIDS NOW
ANYWAY
SO I WAS JUST HANGING OUT IN THE LOUNGEROOM WHEN SEB WALKED PAST ME ON HIS WAY TO TAKE A SHOWER
AND HE JUST SORT OF... LOOKED AT ME, AND I KNEW.
ANYWAY~ I FOLLOWED HIM INTO THE BATHROOM AND HE GAVE ME A BLOW JOB BY THE WASHING MACHINE.

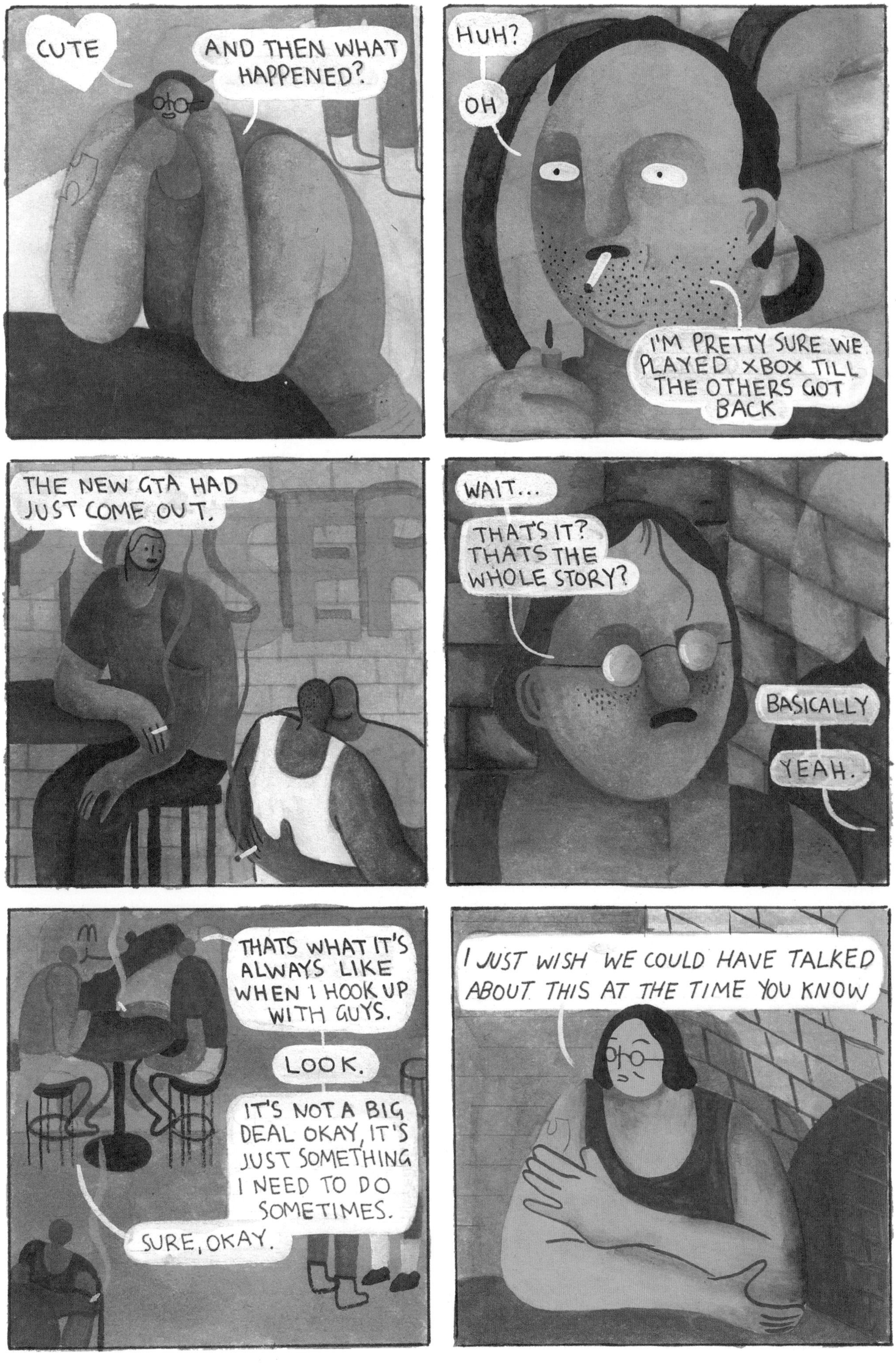
CUTE
AND THEN WHAT HAPPENED?
HUH?
OH
I'M PRETTY SURE WE PLAYED XBOX TILL THE OTHERS GOT BACK
THE NEW GTA HAD JUST COME OUT.
WAIT...
THAT'S IT? THATS THE WHOLE STORY?
BASICALLY
YEAH.
THATS WHAT IT'S ALWAYS LIKE WHEN I HOOK UP WITH GUYS.
LOOK.
IT'S NOT A BIG DEAL OKAY, IT'S JUST SOMETHING I NEED TO DO SOMETIMES.
SURE, OKAY.
I JUST WISH WE COULD HAVE TALKED ABOUT THIS AT THE TIME YOU KNOW

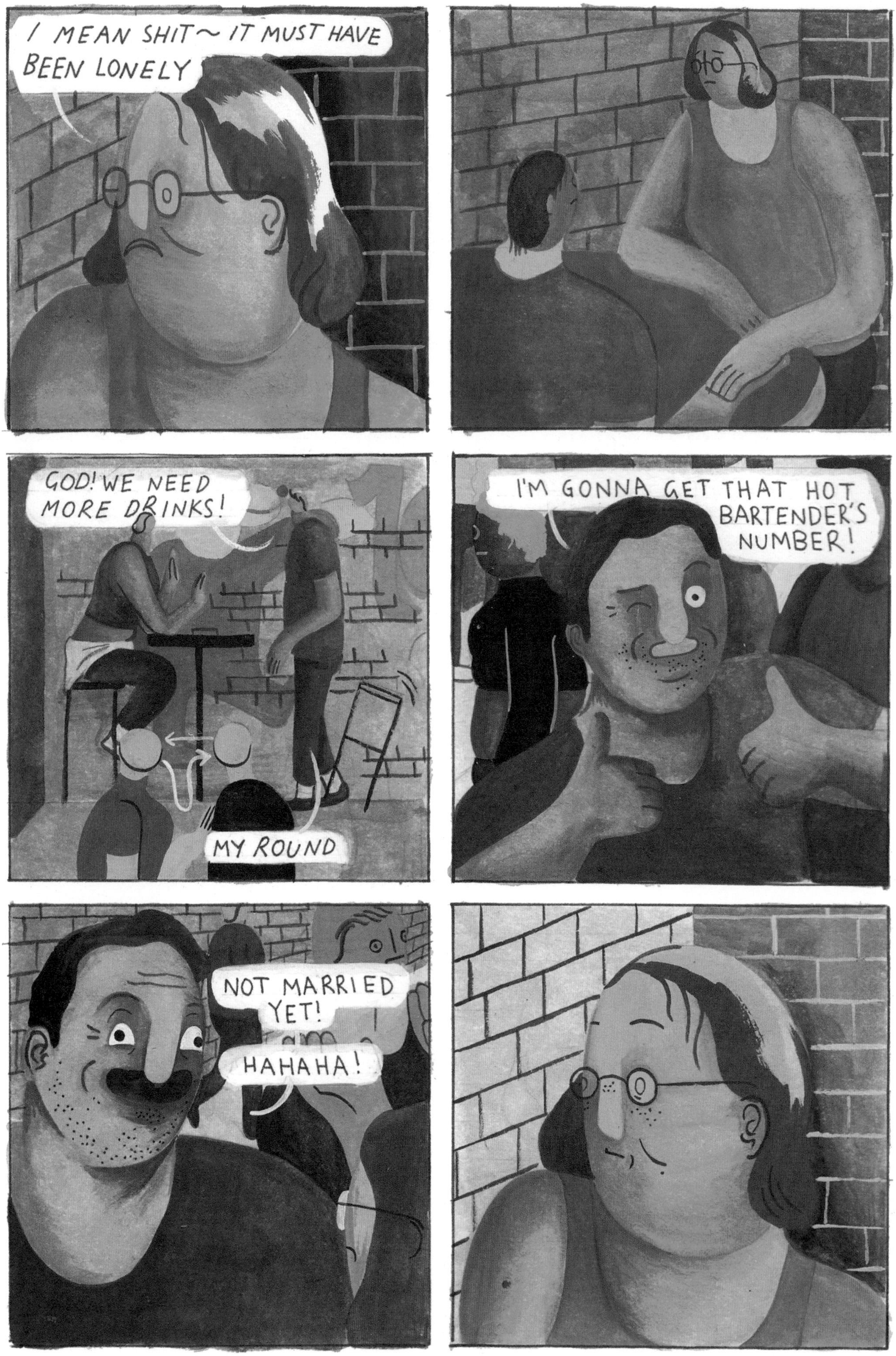
I MEAN SHIT~ IT MUST HAVE BEEN LONELY
GOD! WE NEED MORE DRINKS!
MY ROUND
I'M GONNA GET THAT HOT BARTENDER'S NUMBER!
NOT MARRIED YET!
HAHAHA!

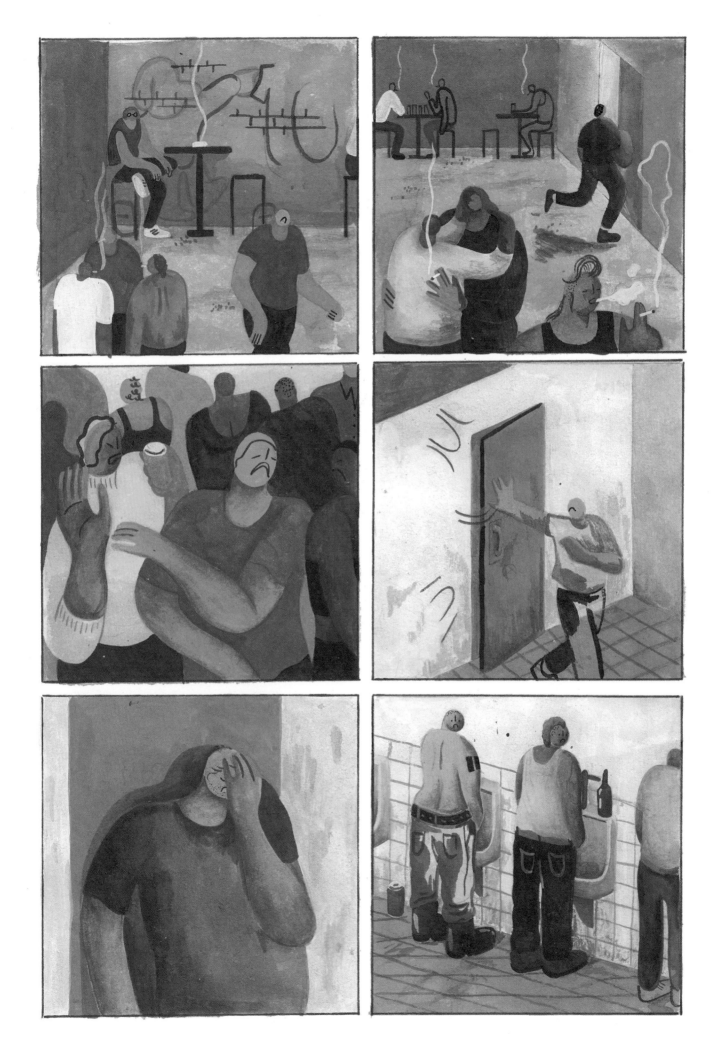

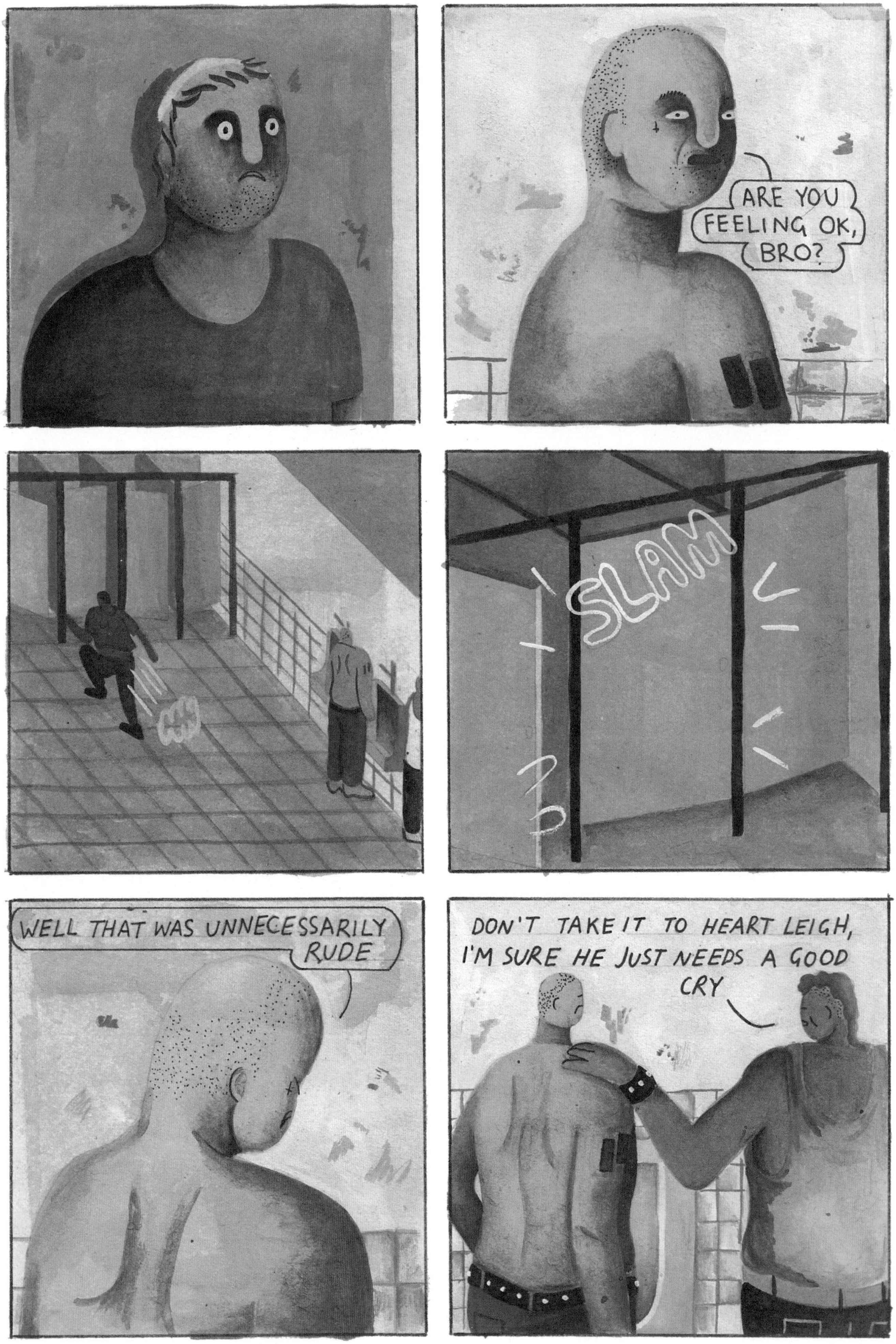
ARE YOU FEELING OK, BRO?
SLAM
WELL THAT WAS UNNECESSARILY RUDE
DON'T TAKE IT TO HEART LEIGH, I'M SURE HE JUST NEEDS A GOOD CRY

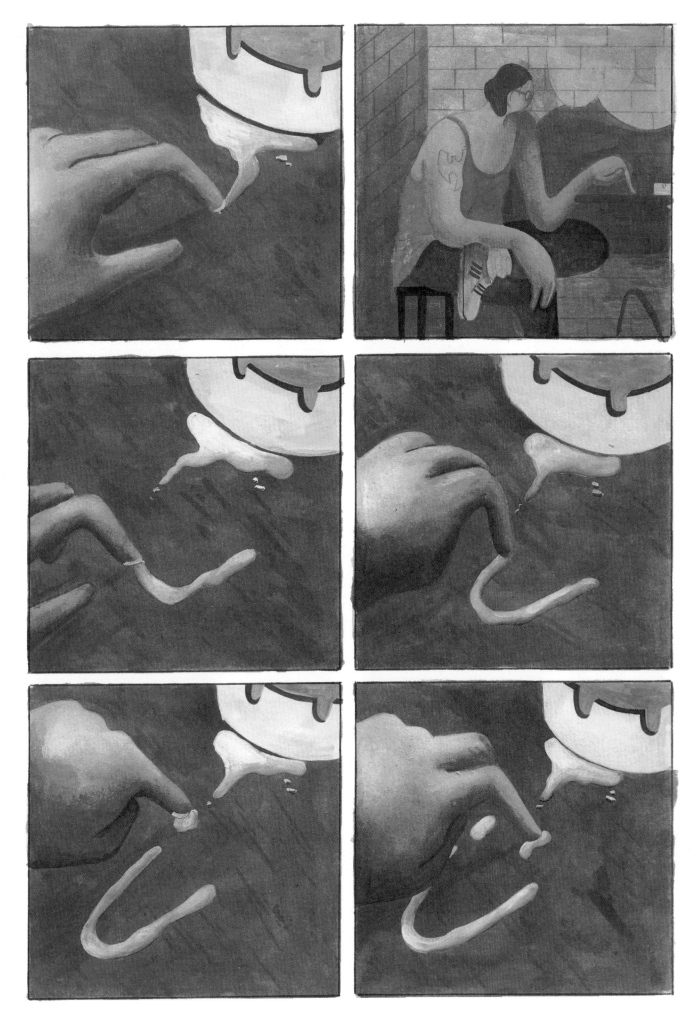

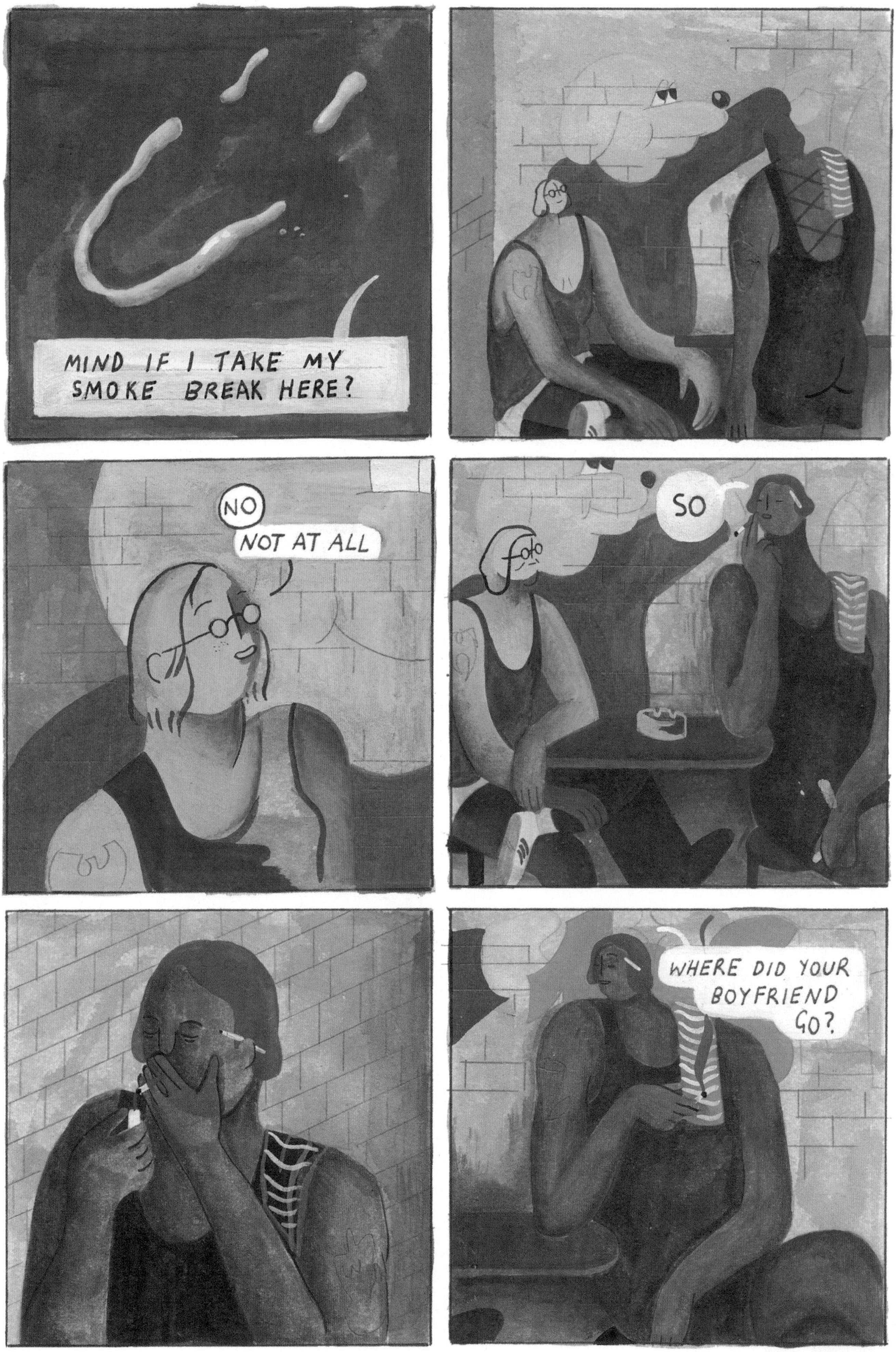
MIND IF I TAKE MY SMOKE BREAK HERE?
NO
NOT AT ALL
SO
WHERE DID YOUR BOYFRIEND GO?

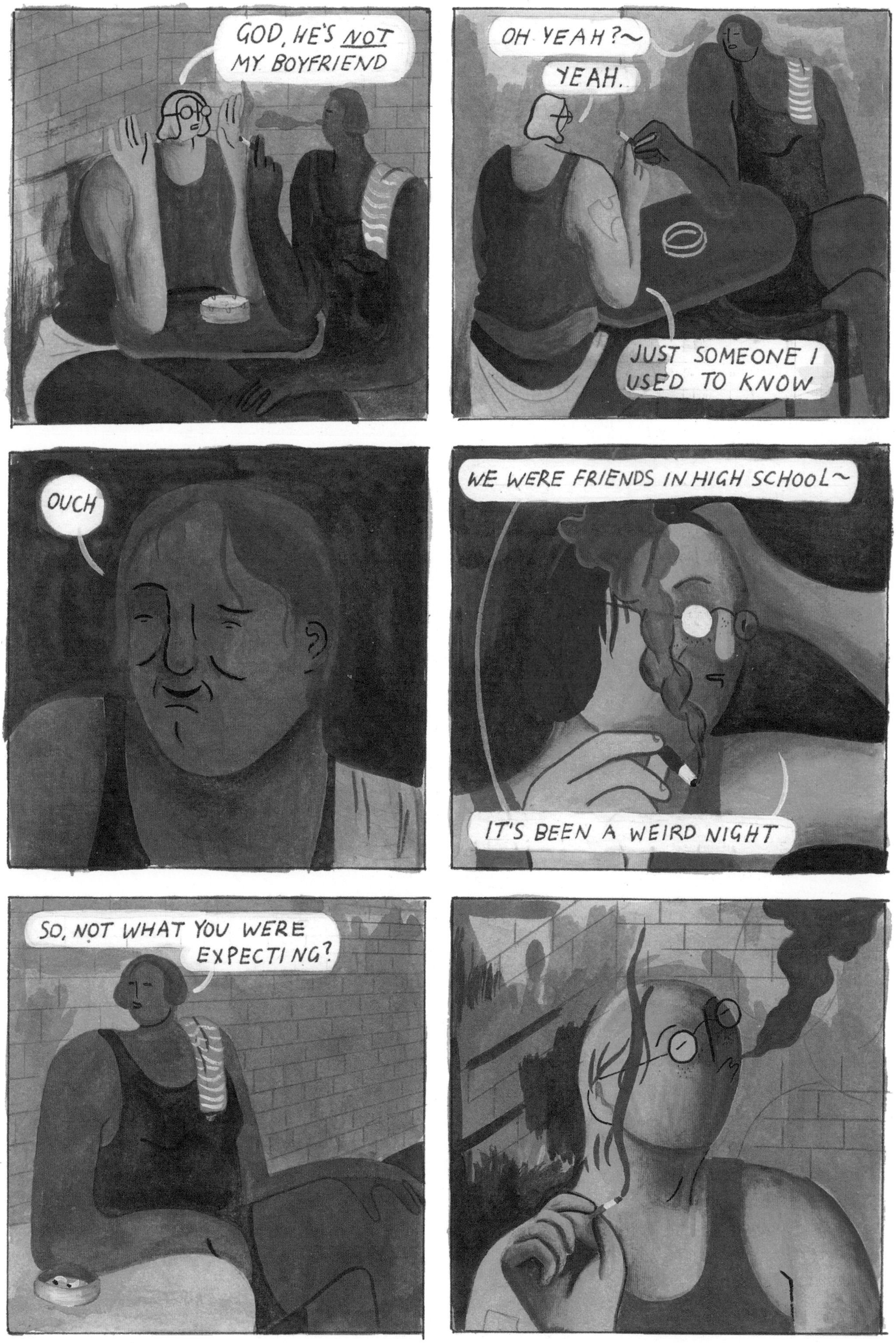
GOD, HE'S NOT MY BOYFRIEND
OH YEAH?~
YEAH.
JUST SOMEONE I USED TO KNOW
OUCH
WE WERE FRIENDS IN HIGH SCHOOL~
IT'S BEEN A WEIRD NIGHT
SO, NOT WHAT YOU WERE EXPECTING?

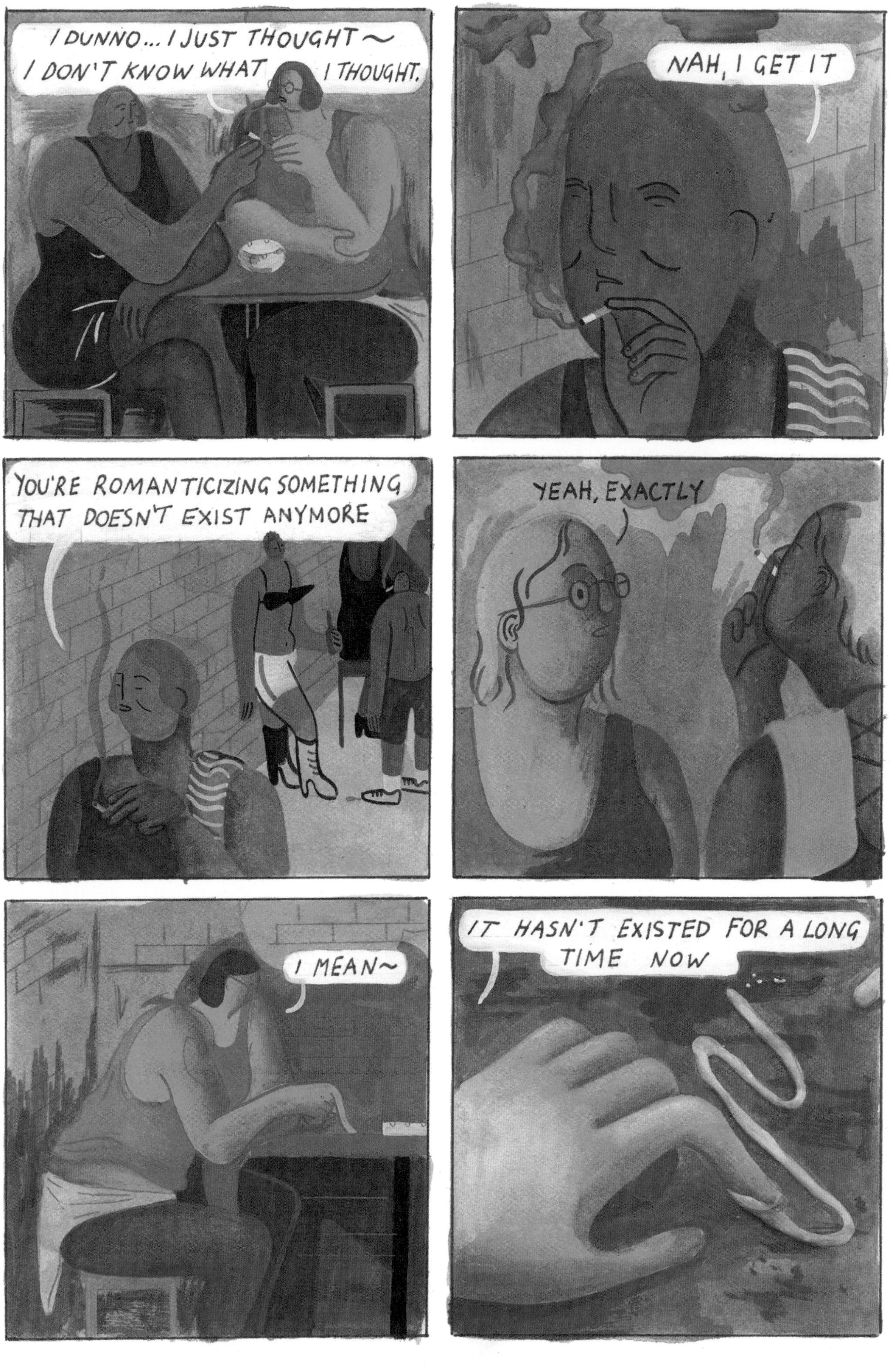
I DUNNO... I JUST THOUGHT~ I DON'T KNOW WHAT I THOUGHT.
NAH, I GET IT
YOU'RE ROMANTICIZING SOMETHING THAT DOESN'T EXIST ANYMORE
YEAH, EXACTLY
I MEAN~
IT HASN'T EXISTED FOR A LONG TIME NOW

I WAS PROBABLY JUST CURIOUS MORE THAN ANYTHING

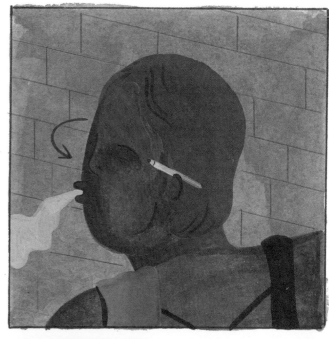

AND WELL~

THAT FRIENDSHIP WAS MY WHOLE WORLD ONCE

PEOPLE CHANGE.

I MEAN... YEAH

IDEALLY

BUT HE'S THE SAME, EXACTLY THE SAME~

ONLY NOW HE'S A TEENAGE BOY IN AN ADULT'S BODY.

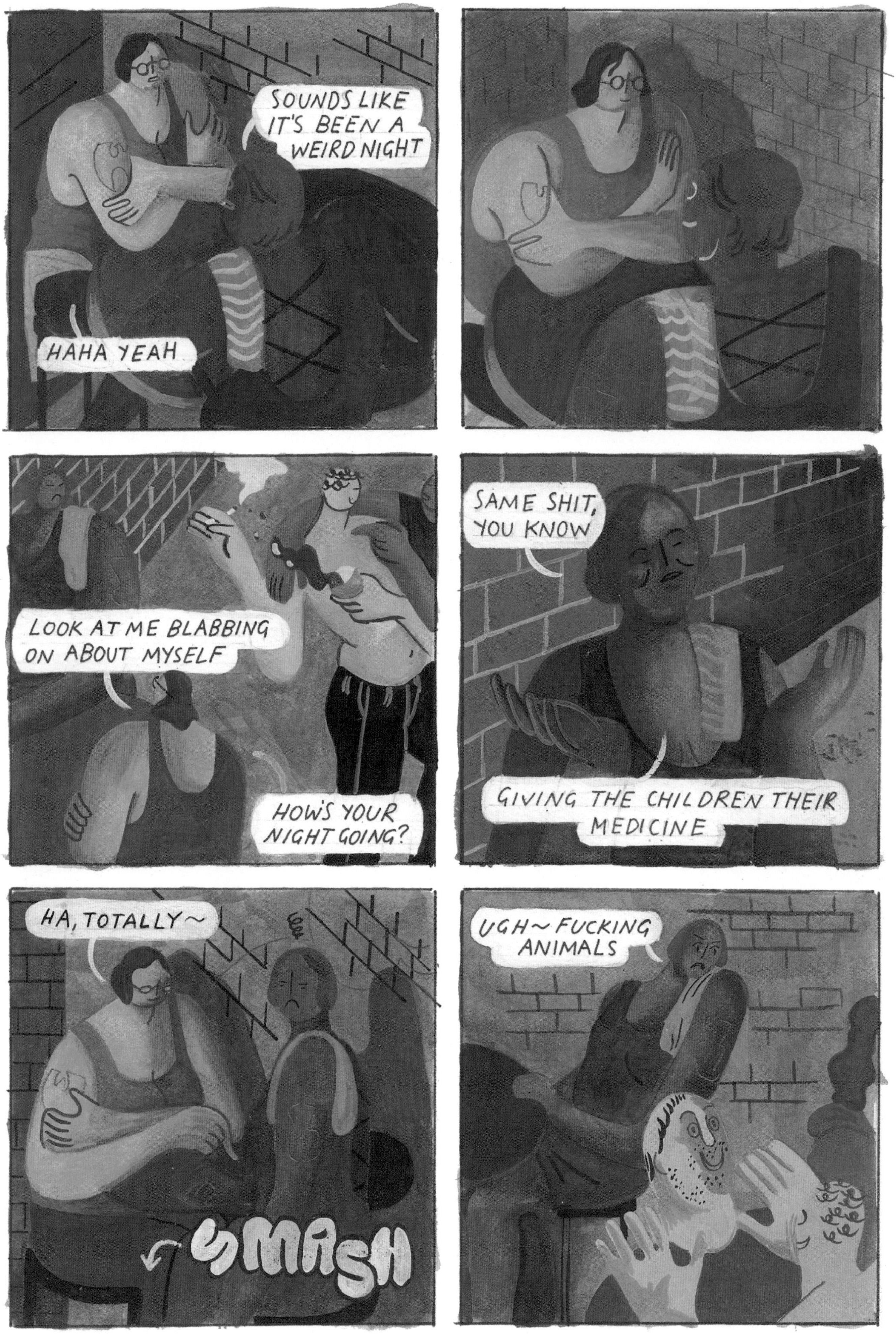
SOUNDS LIKE IT'S BEEN A WEIRD NIGHT
HAHA YEAH
LOOK AT ME BLABBING ON ABOUT MYSELF
HOW'S YOUR NIGHT GOING?
SAME SHIT, YOU KNOW
GIVING THE CHILDREN THEIR MEDICINE
HA, TOTALLY ~
SMASH
UGH ~ FUCKING ANIMALS

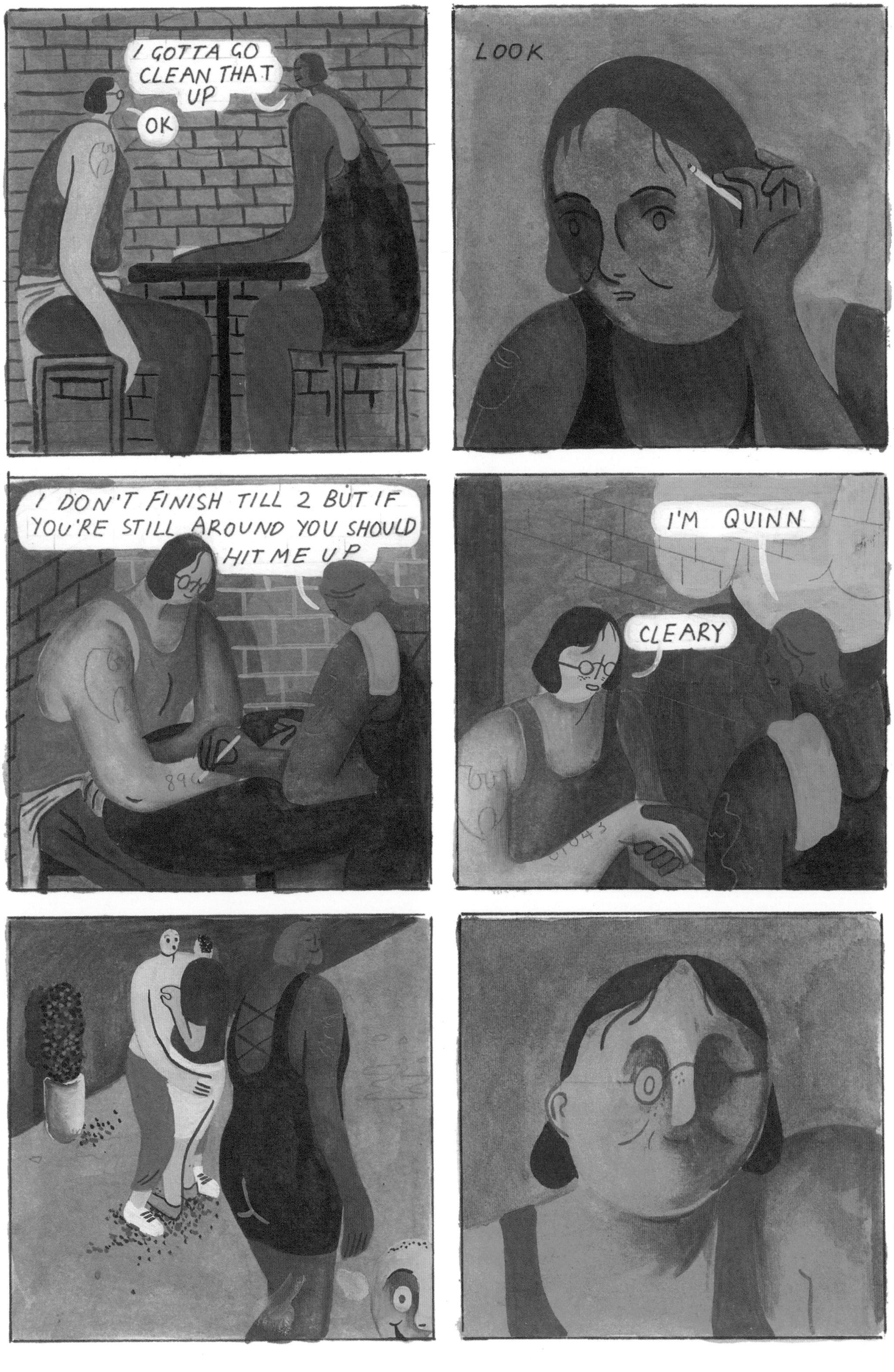
I GOTTA GO CLEAN THAT UP
OK
LOOK
I DON'T FINISH TILL 2 BUT IF YOU'RE STILL AROUND YOU SHOULD HIT ME UP
I'M QUINN
CLEARY

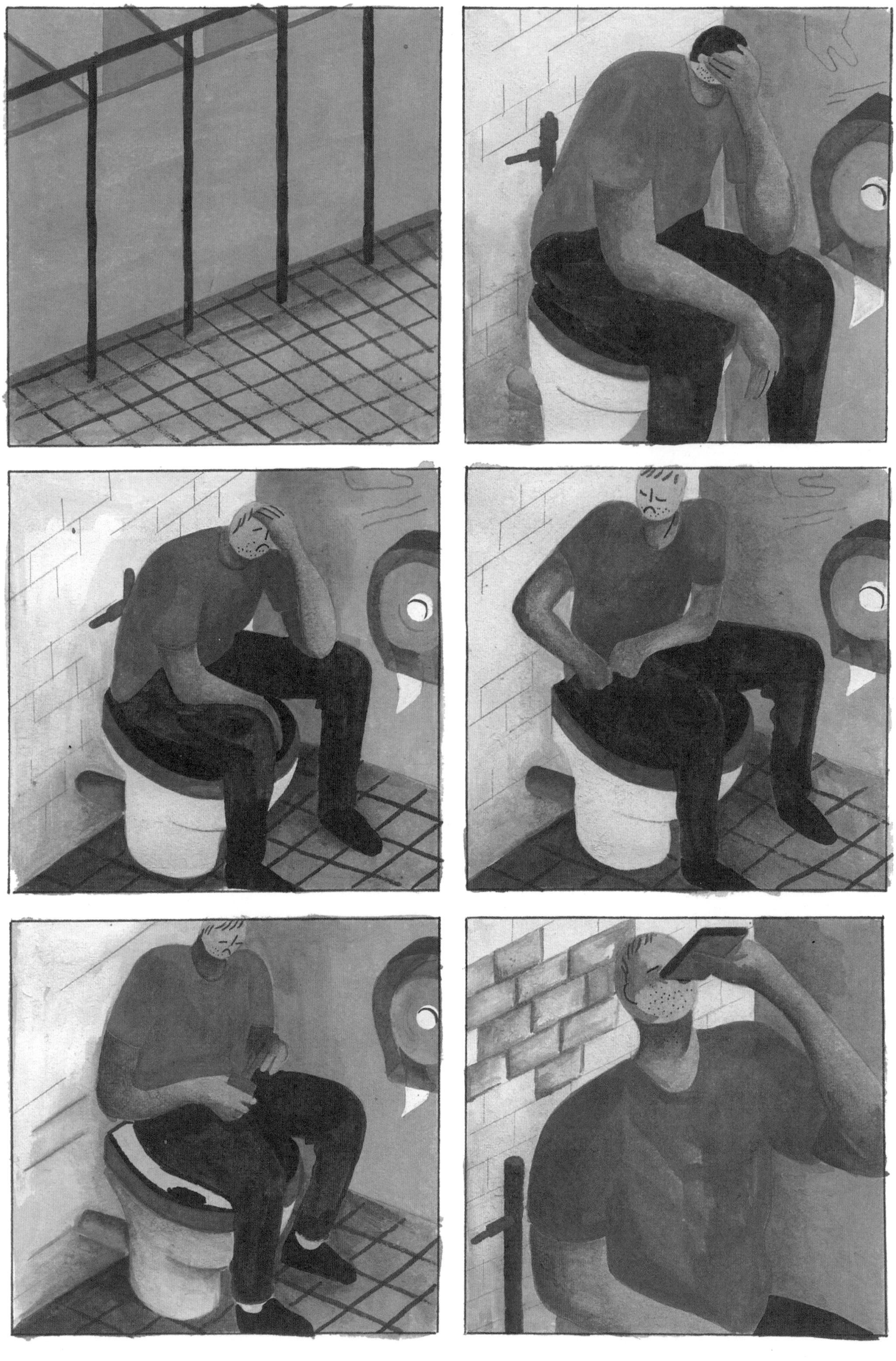

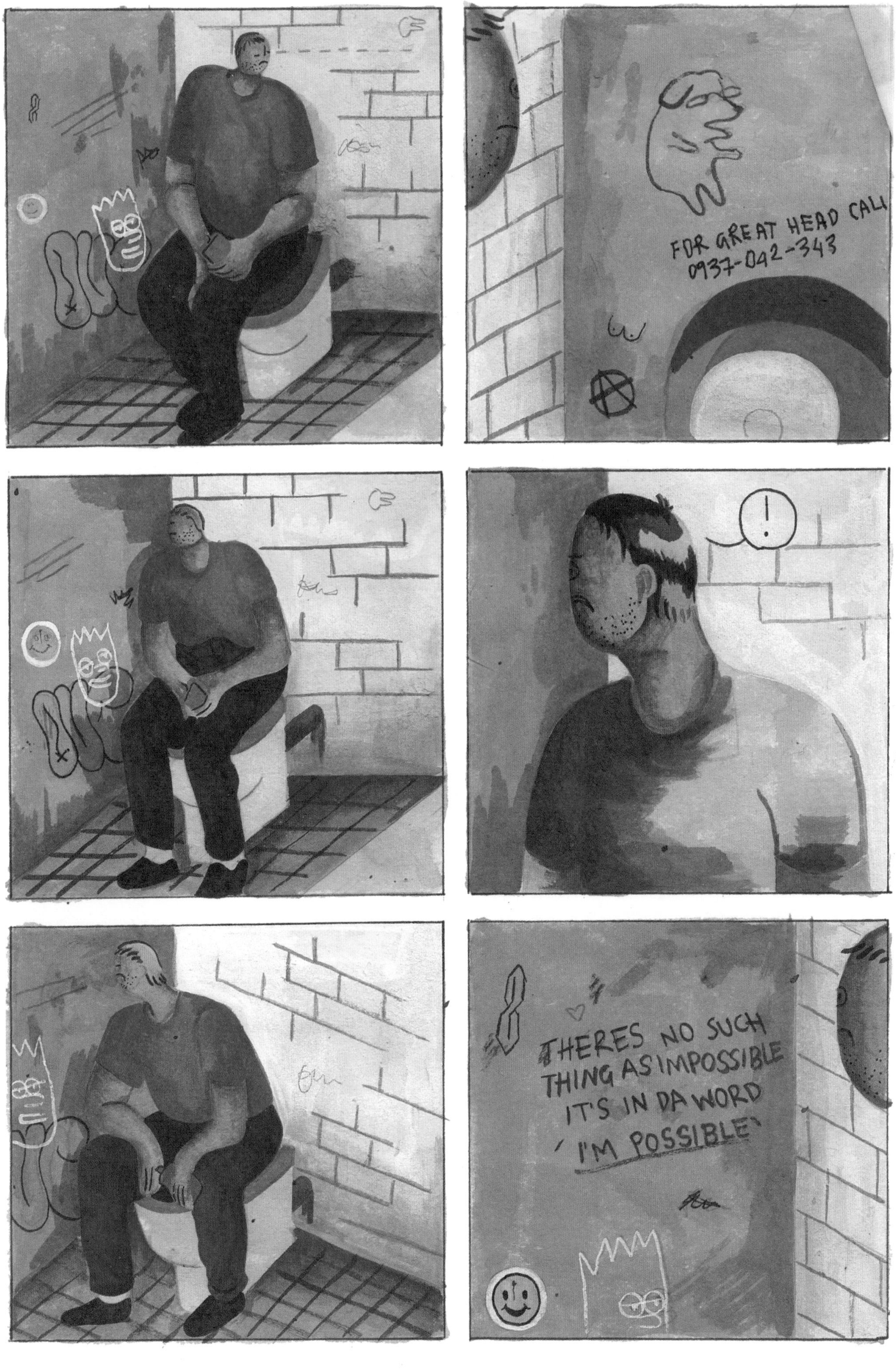
FOR GREAT HEAD CALL
0937-042-343
!
THERES NO SUCH THING AS IMPOSSIBLE IT'S IN DA WORD 'I'M POSSIBLE'

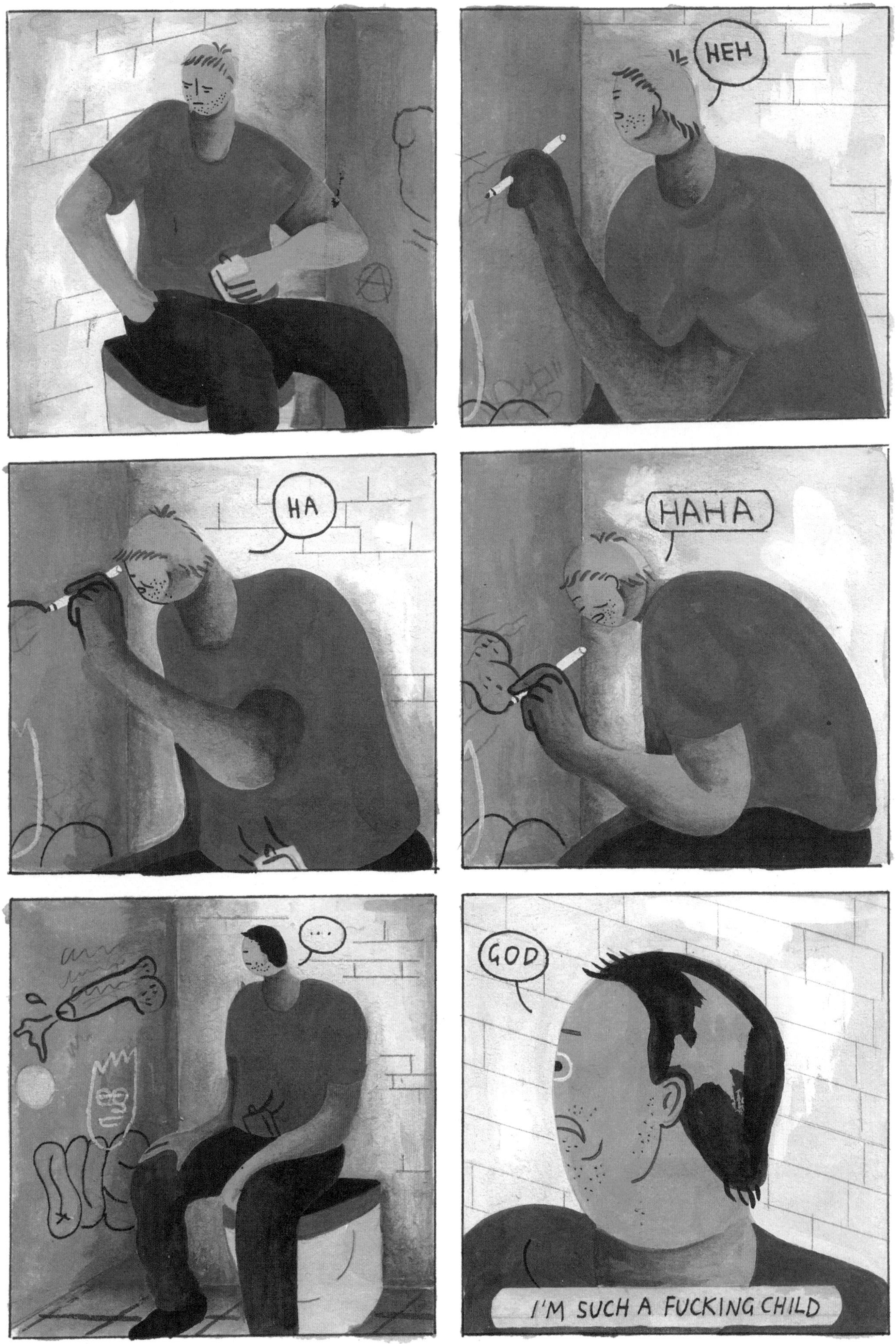
HEH
HA
HAHA
...
GOD
I'M SUCH A FUCKING CHILD

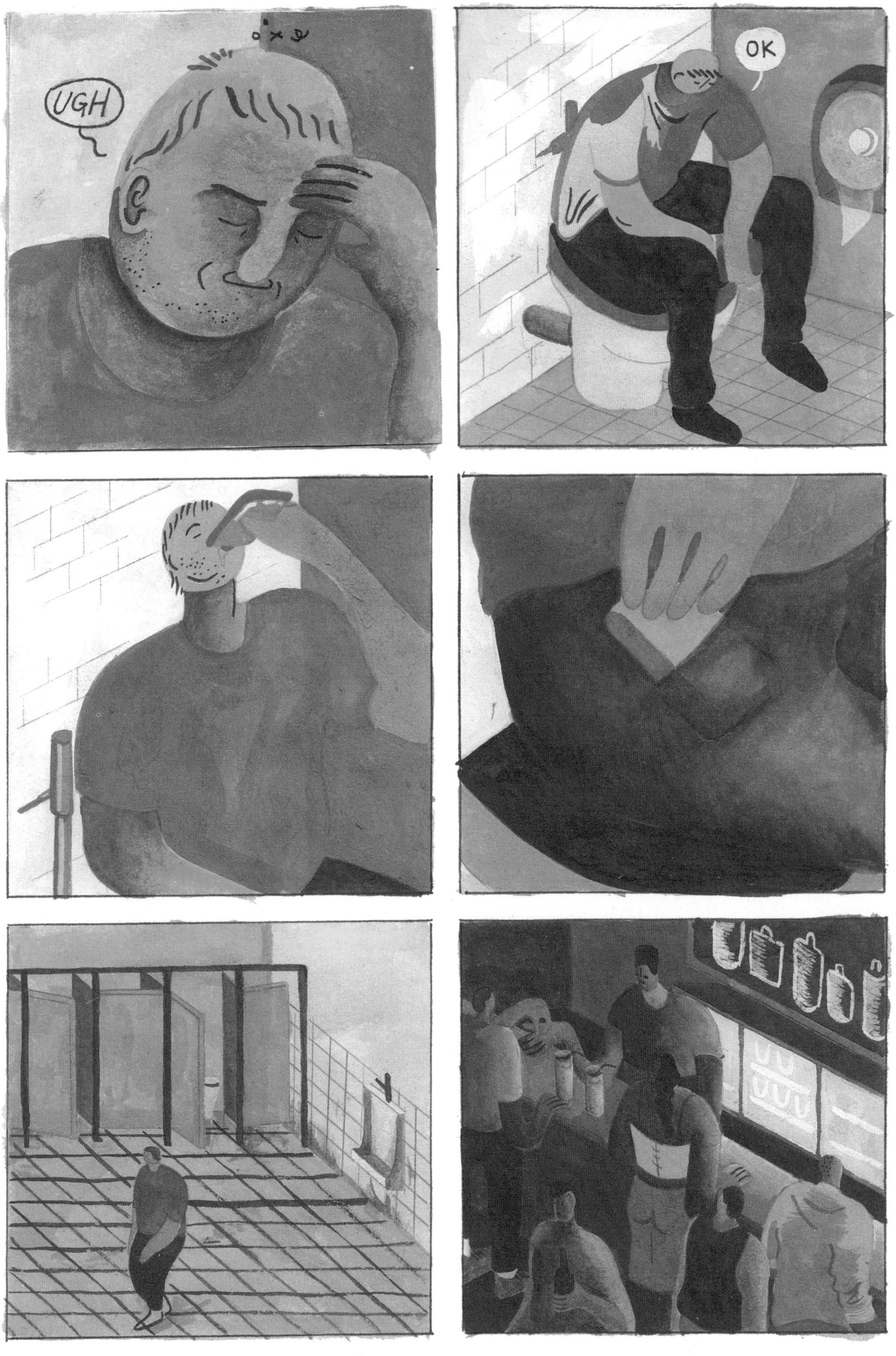
UGH
OK

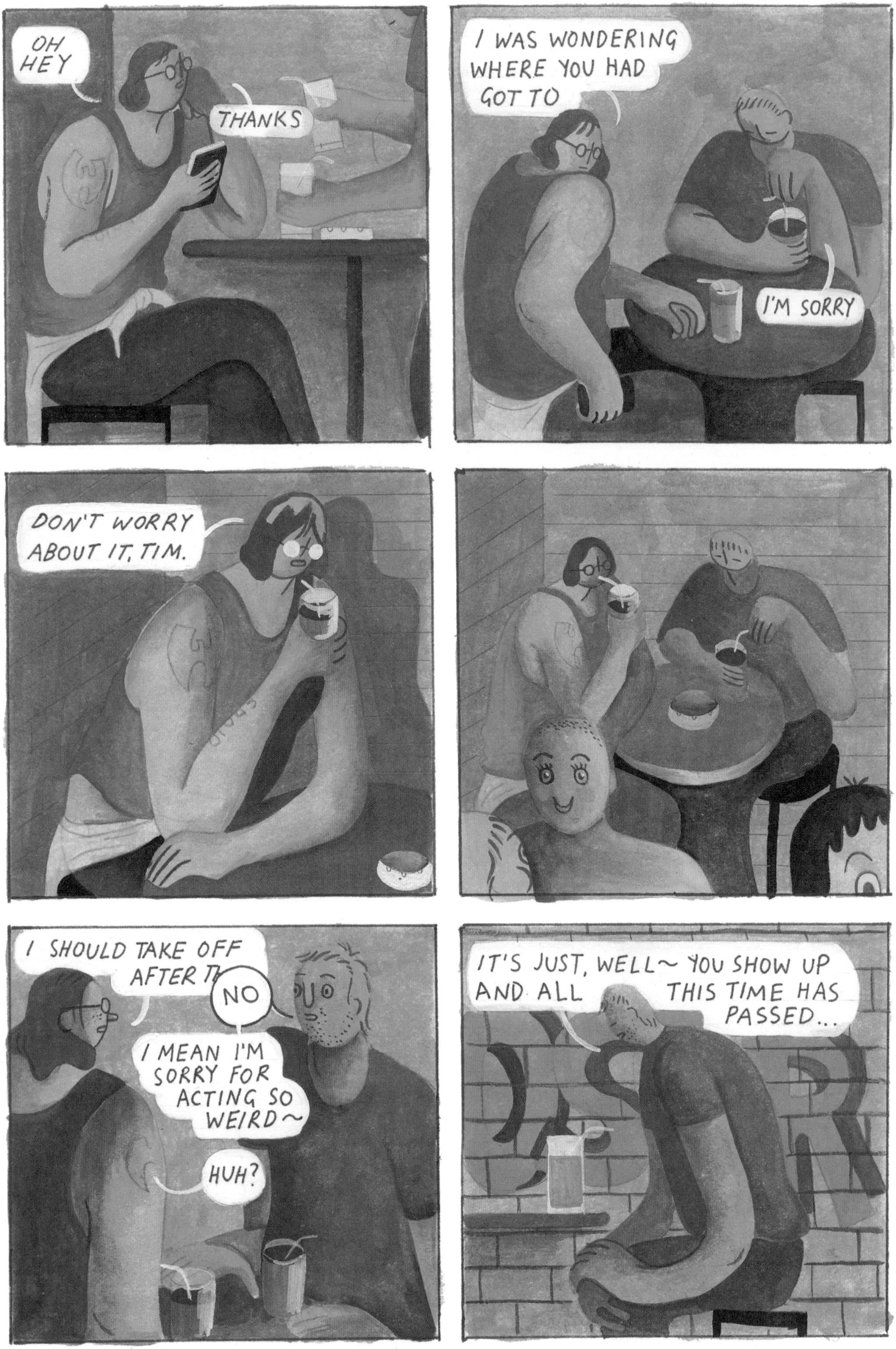
OH HEY
THANKS
I WAS WONDERING WHERE YOU HAD GOT TO
I'M SORRY
DON'T WORRY ABOUT IT, TIM.
I SHOULD TAKE OFF AFTER TH
NO
I MEAN I'M SORRY FOR ACTING SO WEIRD~
HUH?
IT'S JUST, WELL~ YOU SHOW UP AND ALL THIS TIME HAS PASSED...

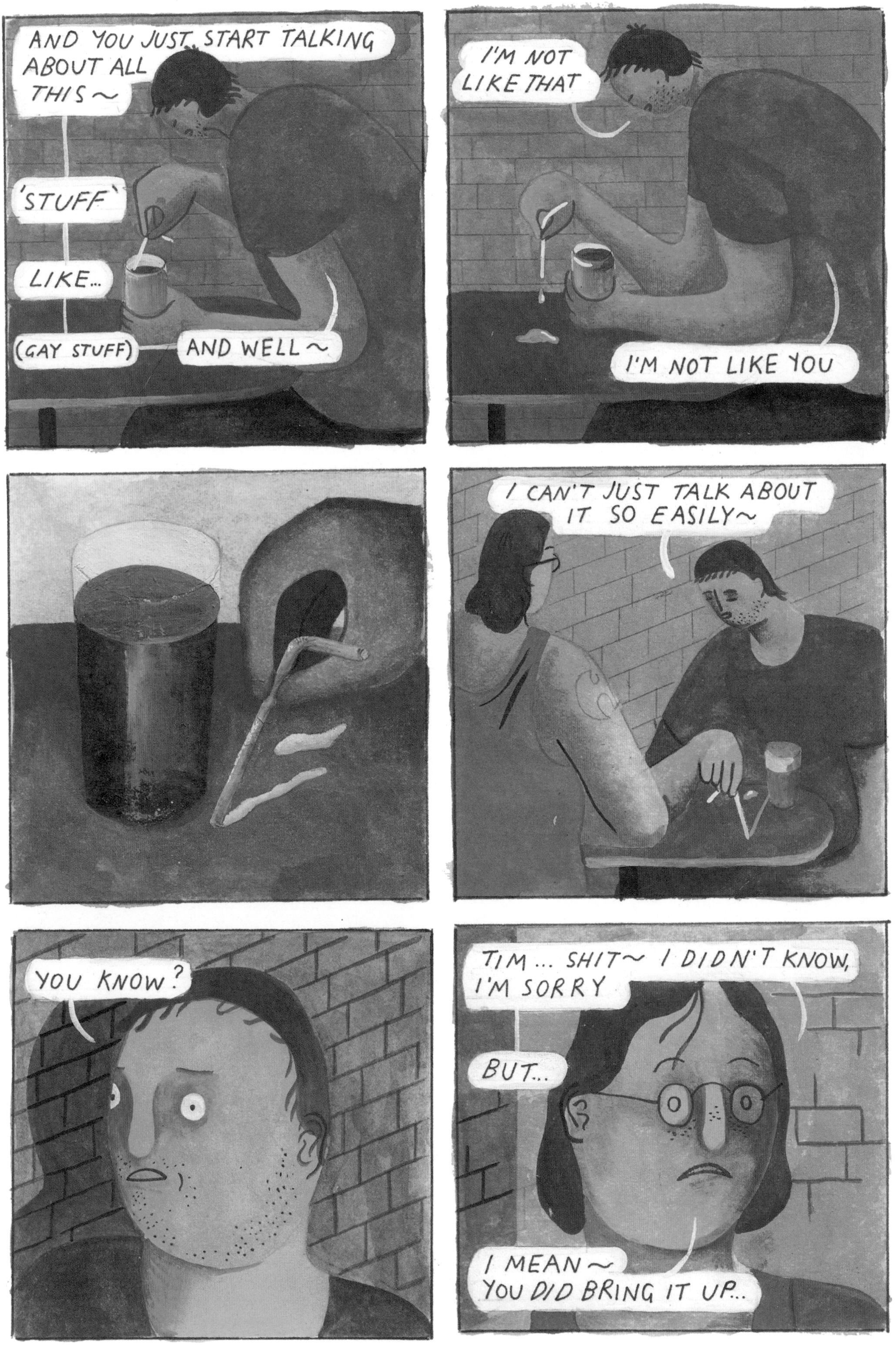
AND YOU JUST START TALKING ABOUT ALL THIS ~
'STUFF'
LIKE...
(GAY STUFF)
AND WELL ~
I'M NOT LIKE THAT
I'M NOT LIKE YOU
I CAN'T JUST TALK ABOUT IT SO EASILY ~
YOU KNOW?
TIM ... SHIT ~ I DIDN'T KNOW, I'M SORRY
BUT...
I MEAN ~ YOU DID BRING IT UP...

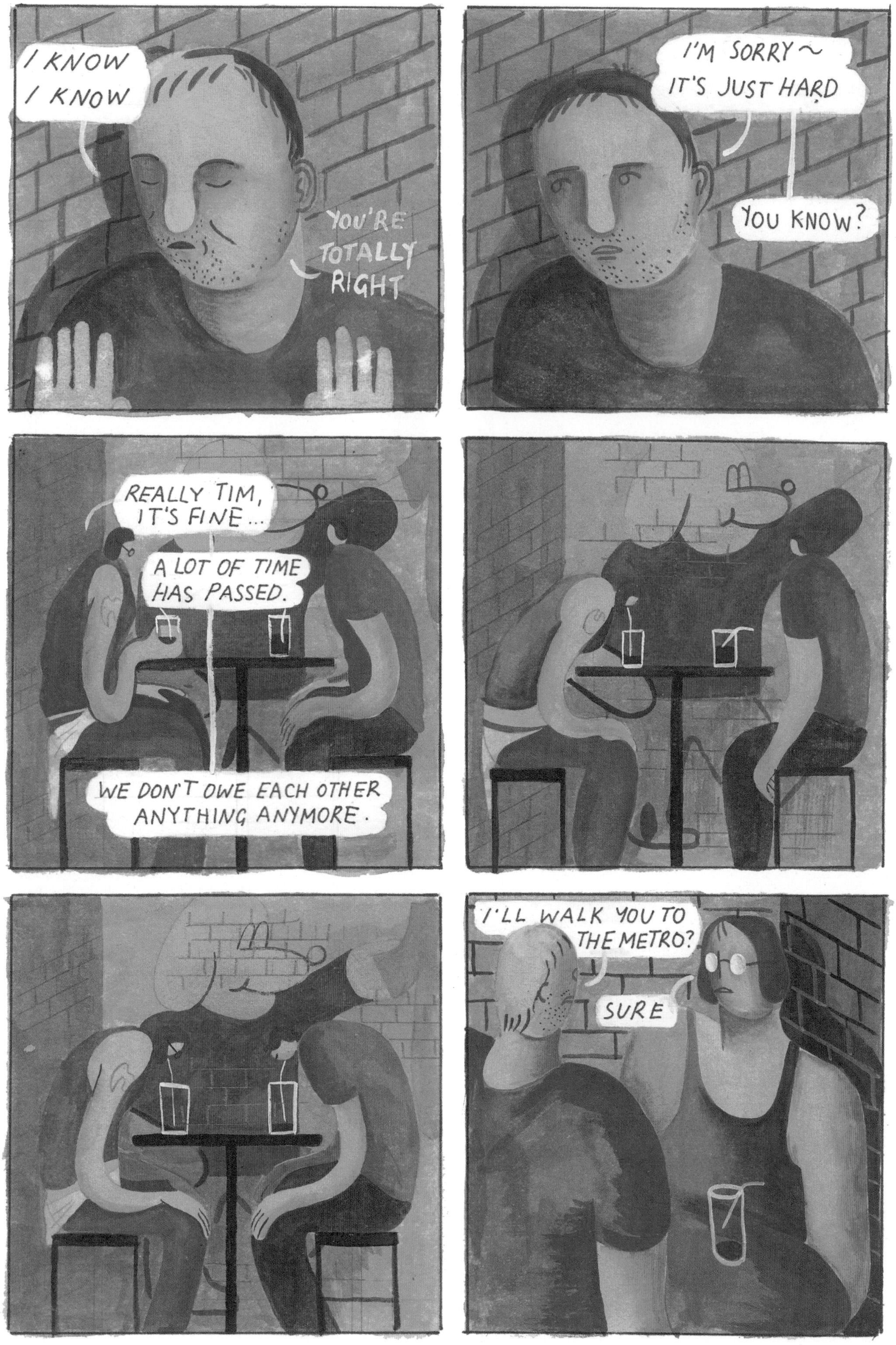
I KNOW
I KNOW
YOU'RE TOTALLY RIGHT
I'M SORRY ~
IT'S JUST HARD
YOU KNOW?
REALLY TIM, IT'S FINE...
A LOT OF TIME HAS PASSED.
WE DON'T OWE EACH OTHER ANYTHING ANYMORE.
I'LL WALK YOU TO THE METRO?
SURE

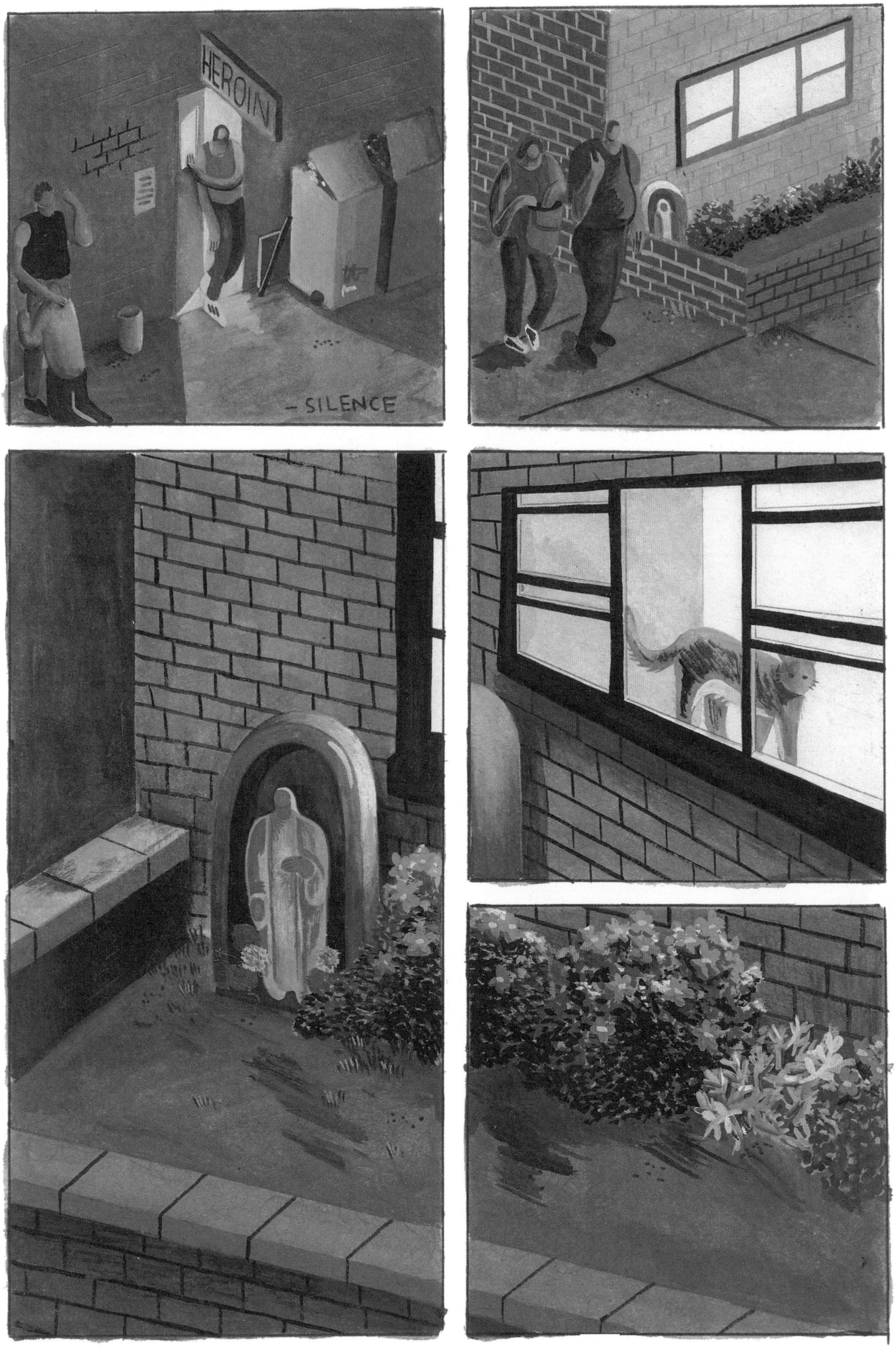
HEROIN
—SILENCE

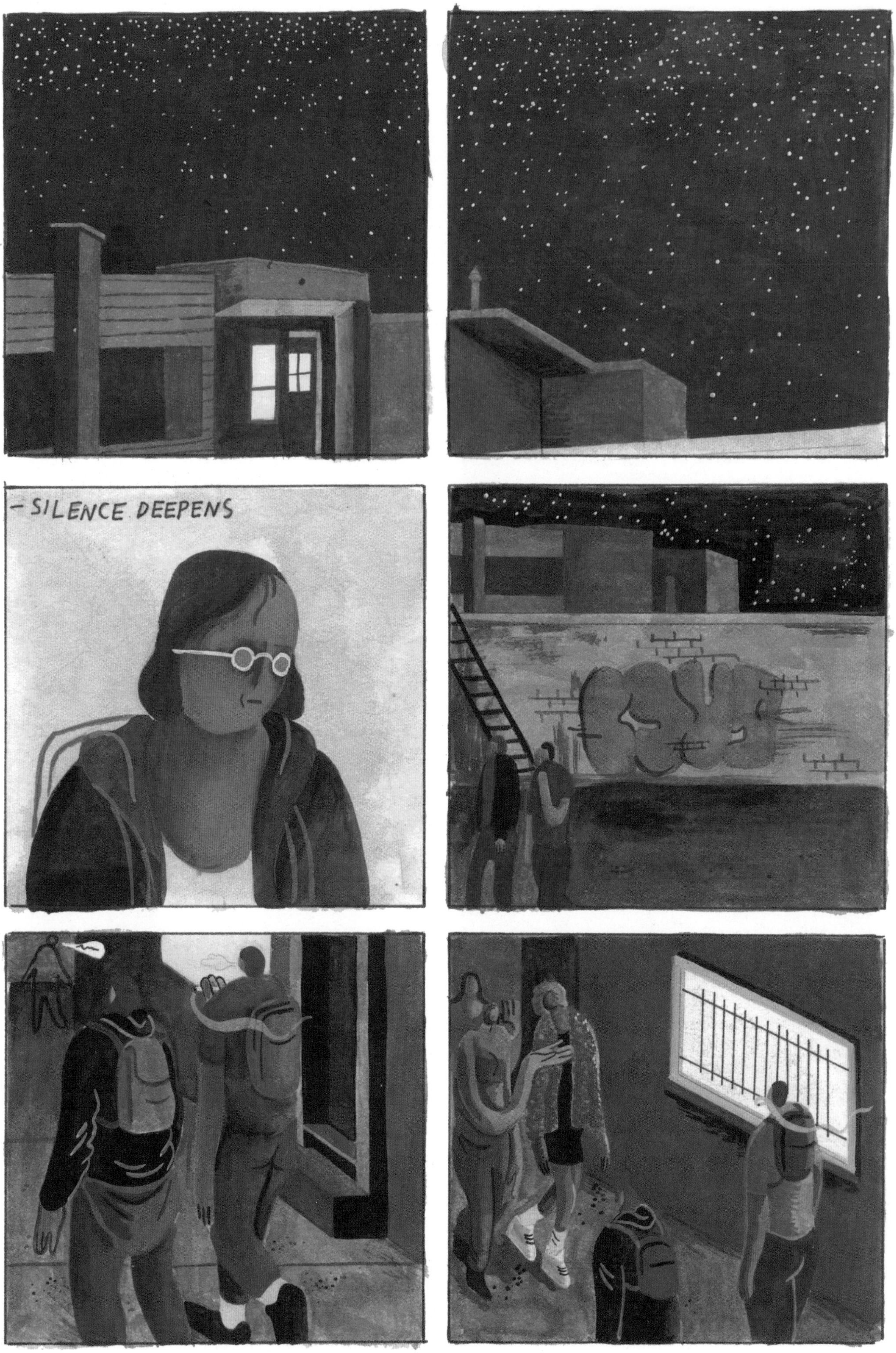
-SILENCE DEEPENS

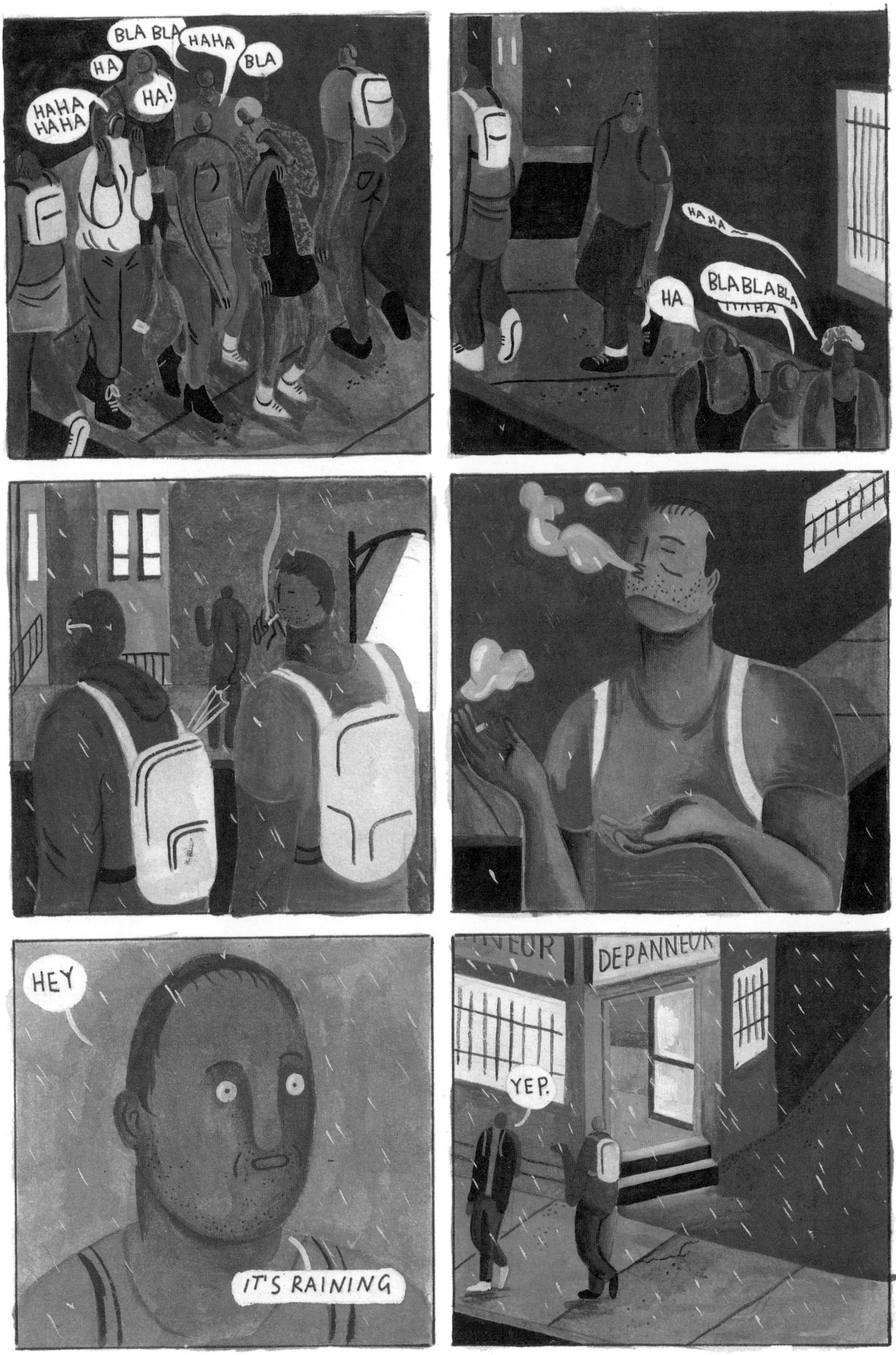
HA
BLA BLA
HAHA
BLA
HAHA HAHA
HA!
HAHA
HA
BLABLABLA
HEY
IT'S RAINING
DEPANNEUR
YEP.

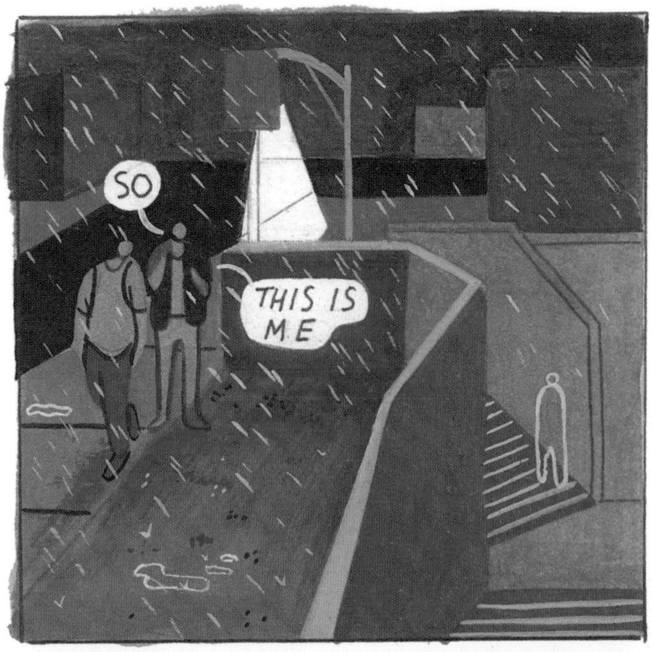
SO
THIS IS ME

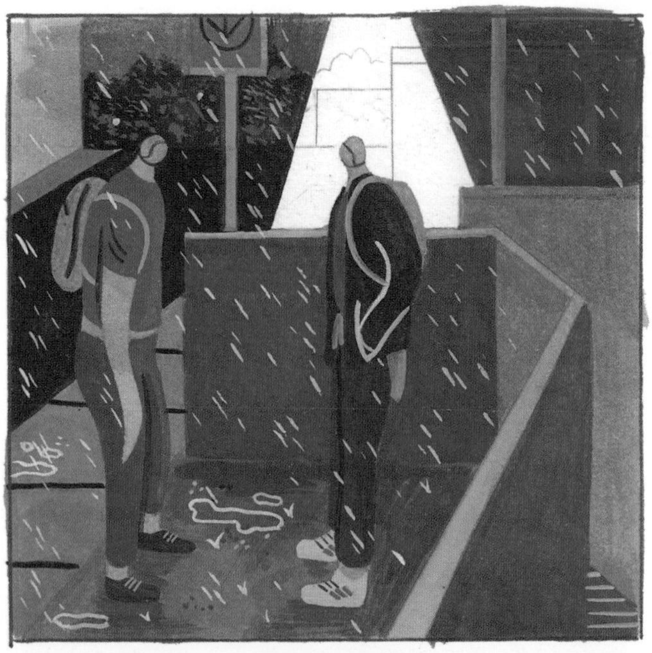

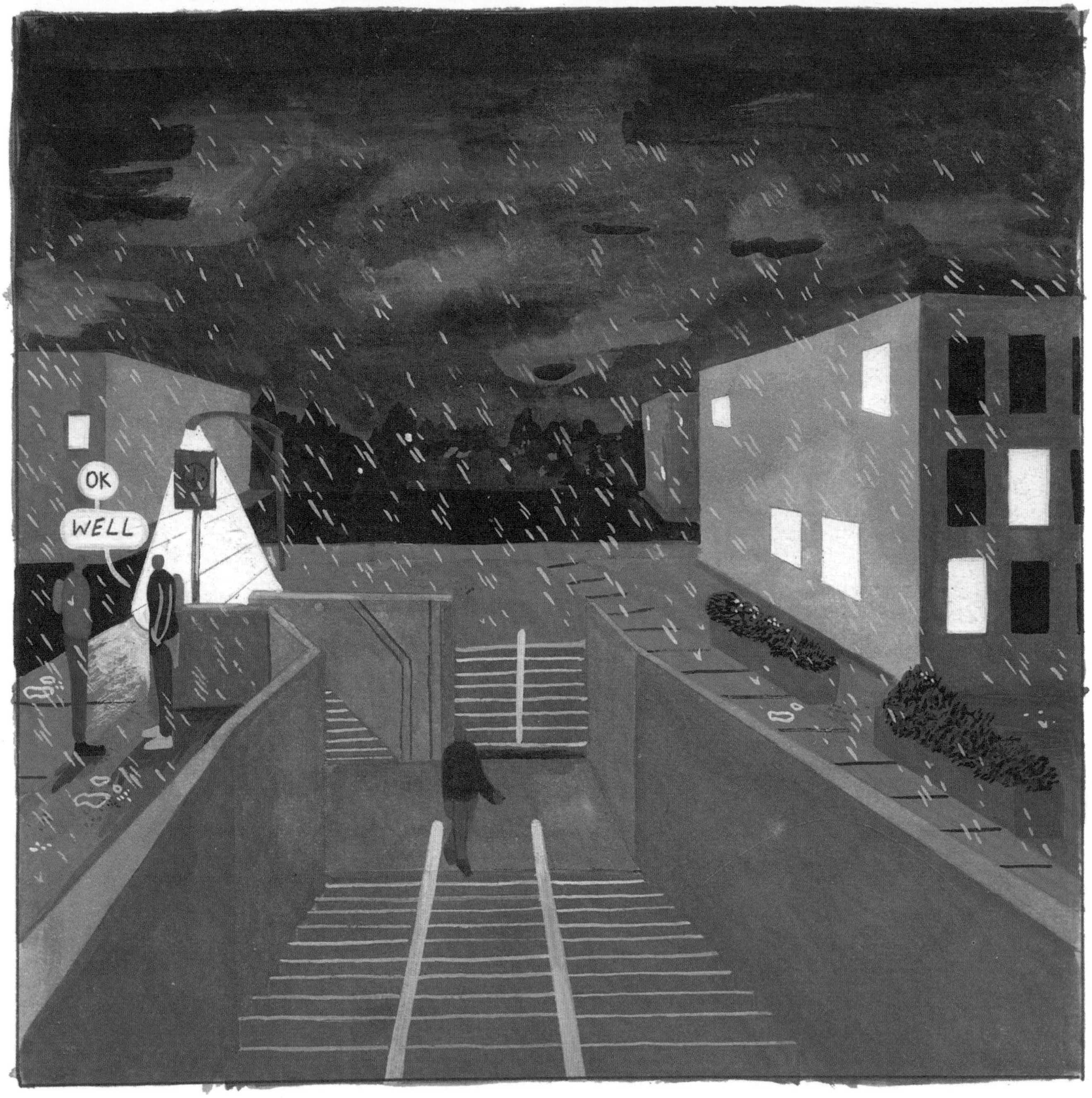
OK
WELL

...
IT WAS COOL RUNNING INTO YOU~
YEAH
FOR SURE
SEE YOU...

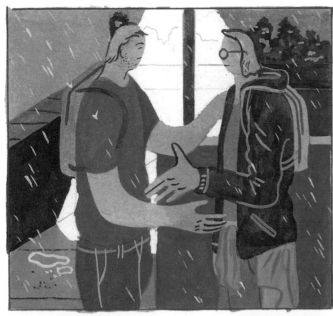

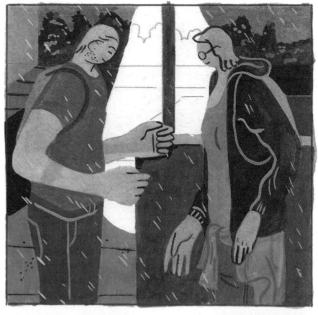

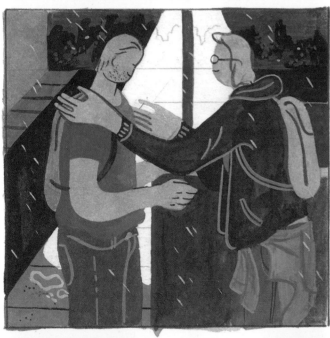

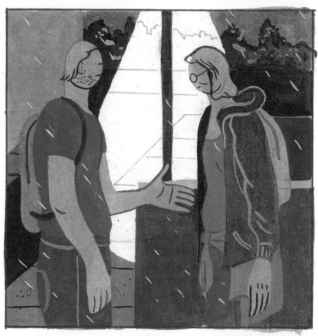

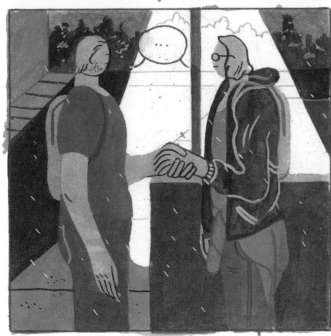

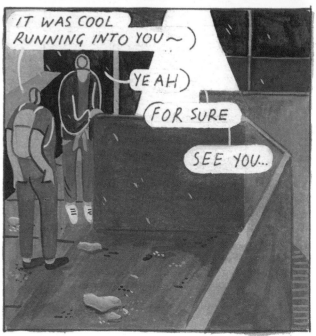

TIM
YEAH?
GOOD LUCK WITH THE WEDDING OK~
OK

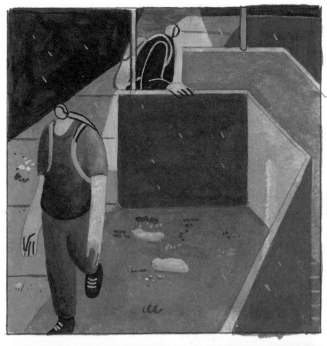

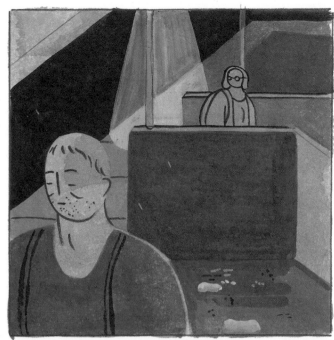

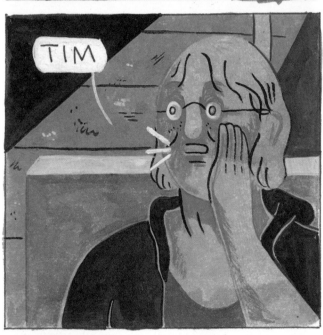

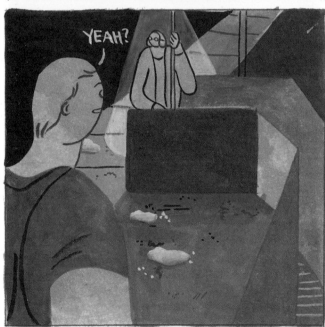

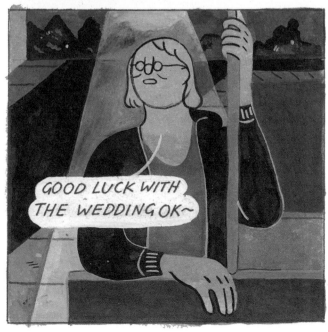

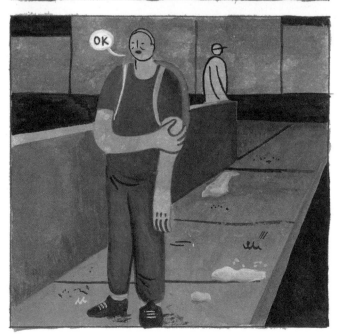

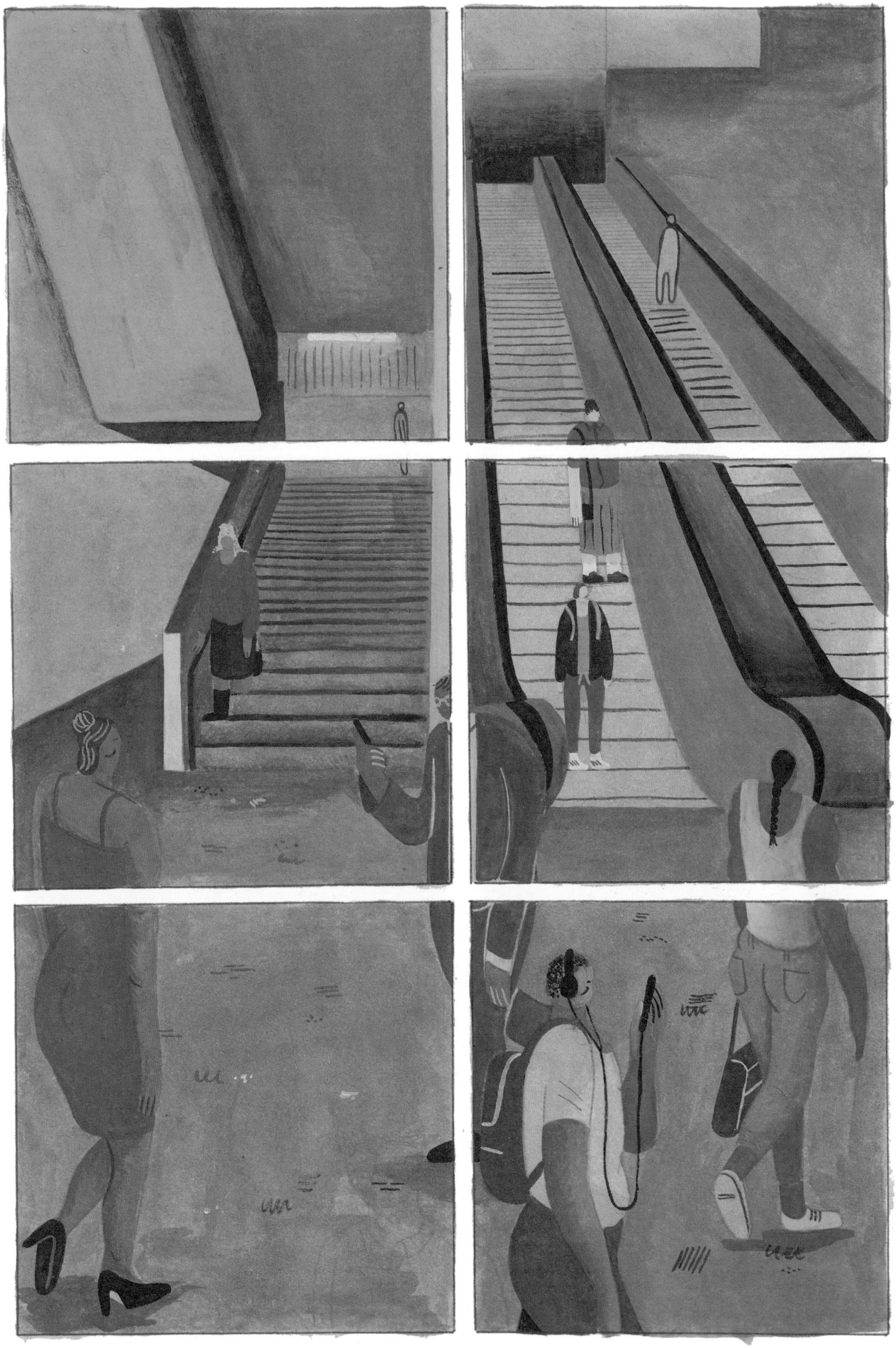

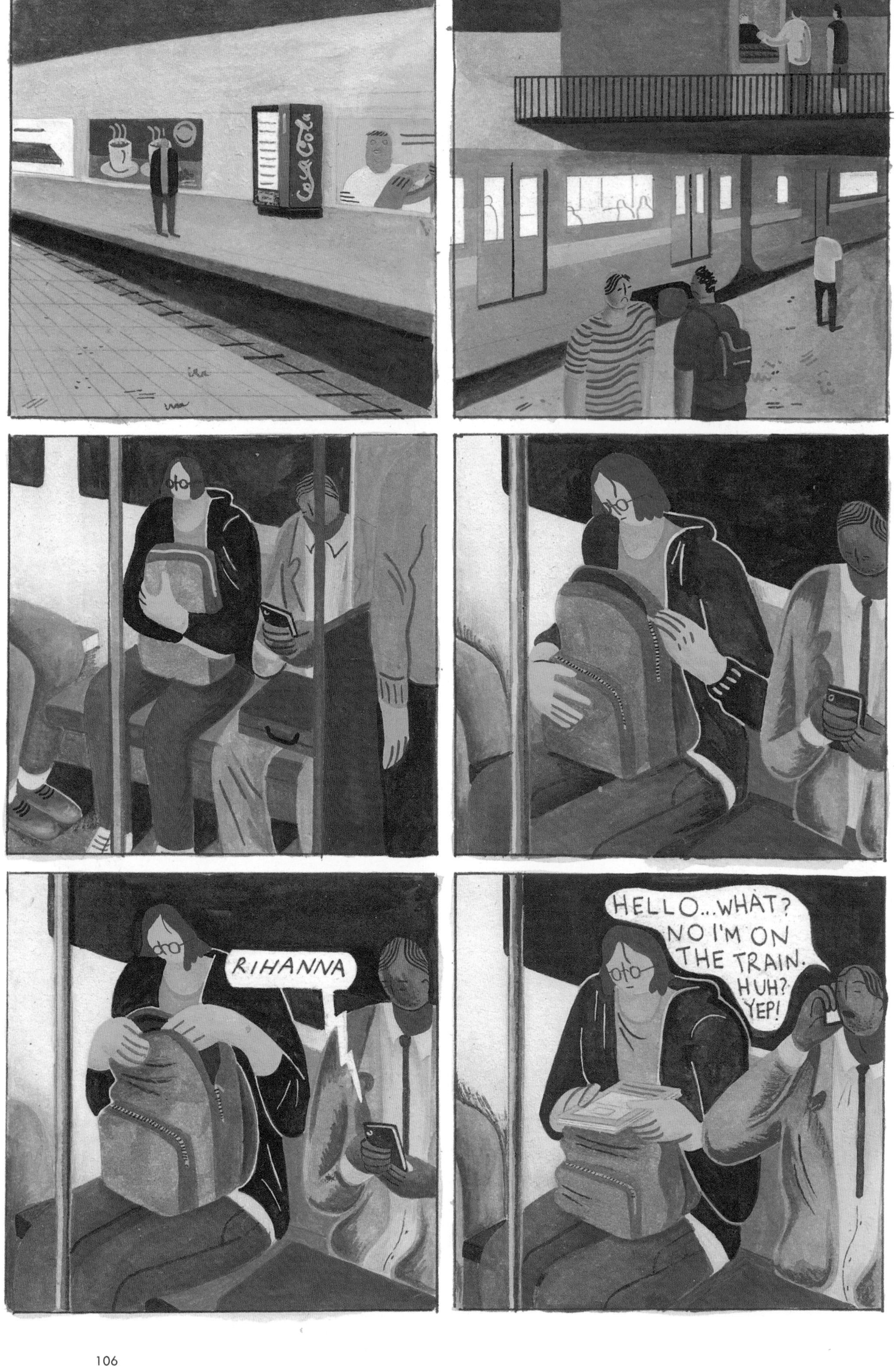
RIHANNA
HELLO...WHAT? NO I'M ON THE TRAIN. HUH? YEP!

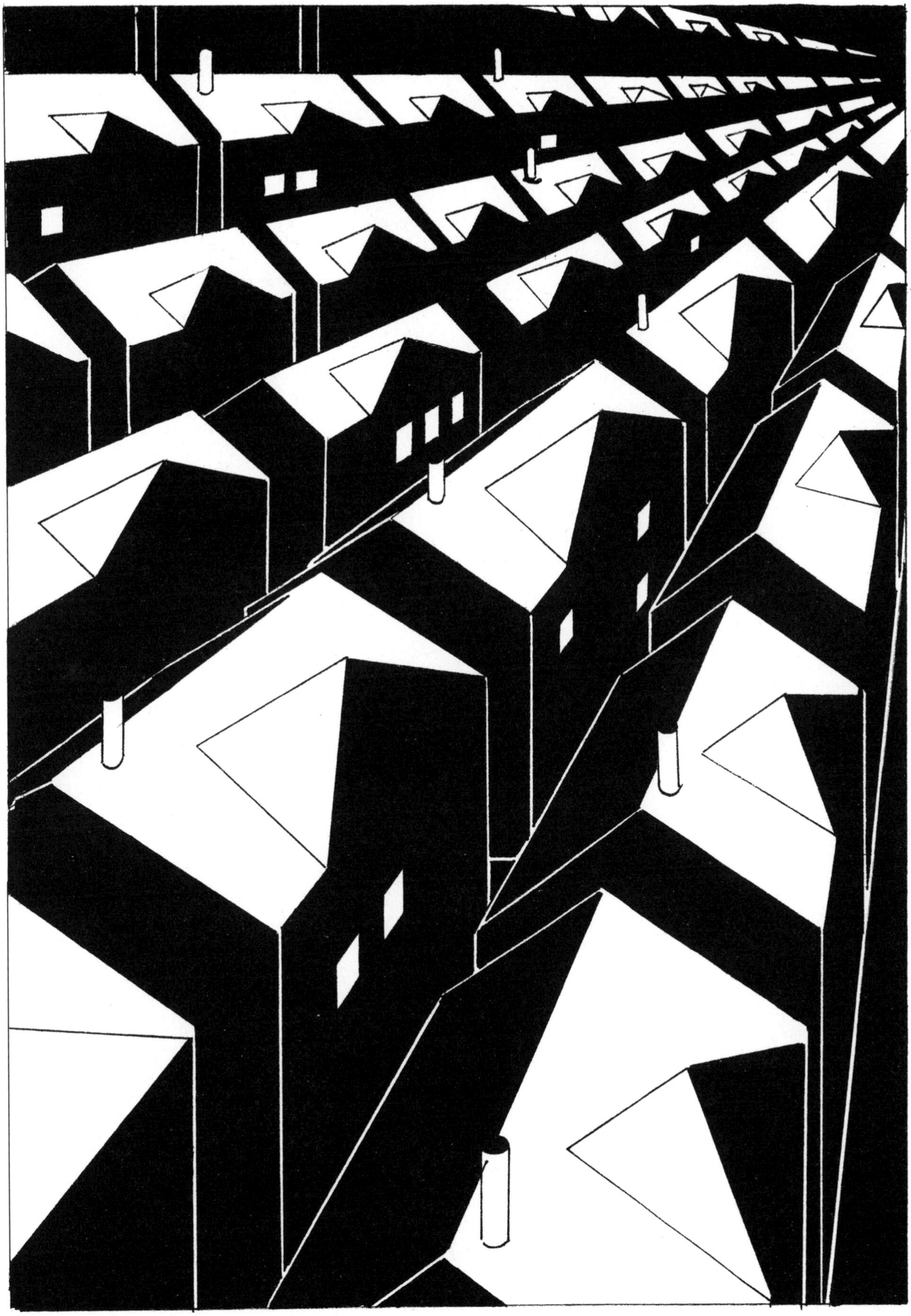

I LOOK AROUND; CAREFULLY PLACED SOUVENIRS FROM FRIENDS AND LOVERS DECORATE MY WALLS. A FEW NEAT PILES OF BOOKS AND CLOTHES TUCKED INTO THE CUBBYHOLES OF A MILK CRATE CLOSET, A HANDMADE DESK CLUTTERED WITH ART SUPPLIES, EVIDENCE OF A LIFE LIVED SIMPLY BUT FULLY.

THEN, WITH THE SUDDEN CLARITY OF A SHARP SLAP,
I SEE WHAT HE MUST SEE.

IN THAT MOMENT, MY LIFE IS FLAYED OF ITS NUANCE AND I AM
LESS THAN REAL. IN HIS GAZE I AM SUDDENLY REDUCED TO A BROKE
STRIPPER LIVING IN A LITTLE ROOM WITH ONLY A FEW
TATTERED POSSESSIONS. I FEEL MYSELF FEELING ASHAMED,
AND FEELING EMBARRASSED.

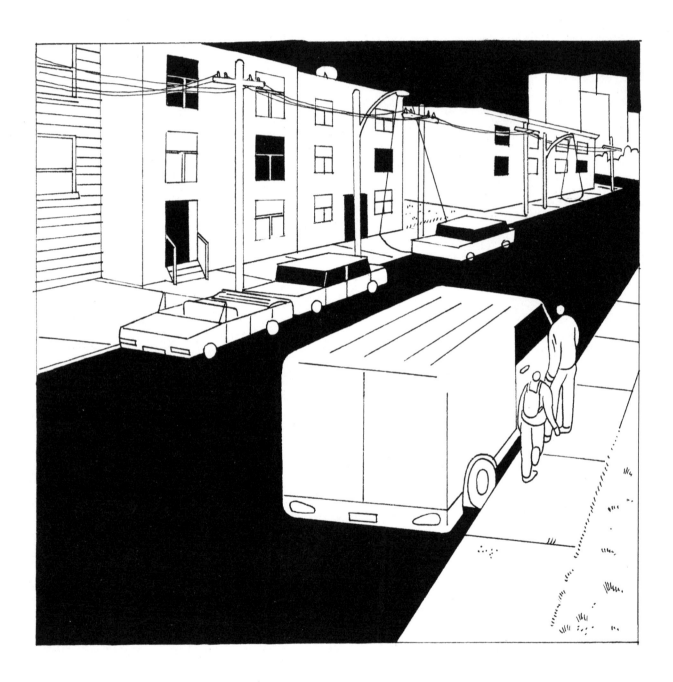

I HATE HIM FOR THAT.

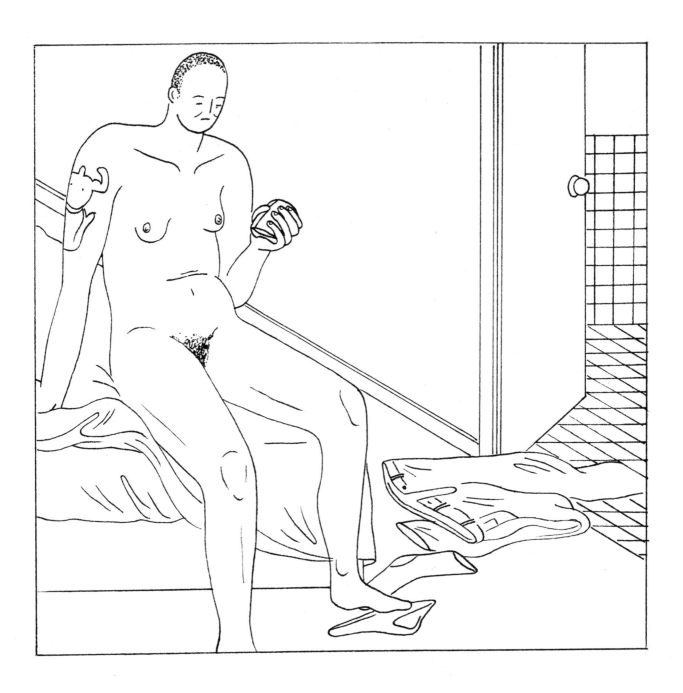

I LET HIM FUCK ME ONE MORE TIME. AGAIN, IT'S TOLERABLE
BUT COLORLESS. AS HE TAKES A SHOWER, I STAND IN HIS
BEDROOM, FEELING THE HEFT OF HIS FAT LEATHER WALLET,
AND I FEEL MY QUIET DISDAIN TURN TO VISCERAL DISGUST.

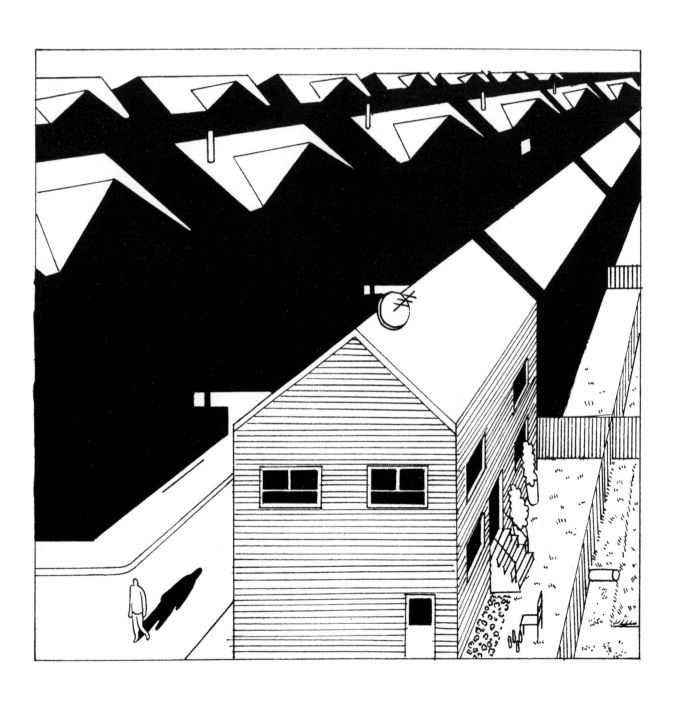

HE'S AS COLORLESS AS THE SEX. FLAT. NOT WORTH REMEMBERING.
MY DISGUST HAS PASSED THROUGH RAGE AND EMERGED AS A
MILITANT INDIFFERENCE.

I PUT DOWN THE WALLET AND DRIFT OUT OF HIS HOUSE

ON THE TRAIN HOME, I DELETE AND BLOCK HIS NUMBER.
MY CURIOSITY WAS SATED. I HAD BEEN EAVESDROPPING ON
A TYPE OF LIFE I HAD NEVER WANTED FOR MYSELF.

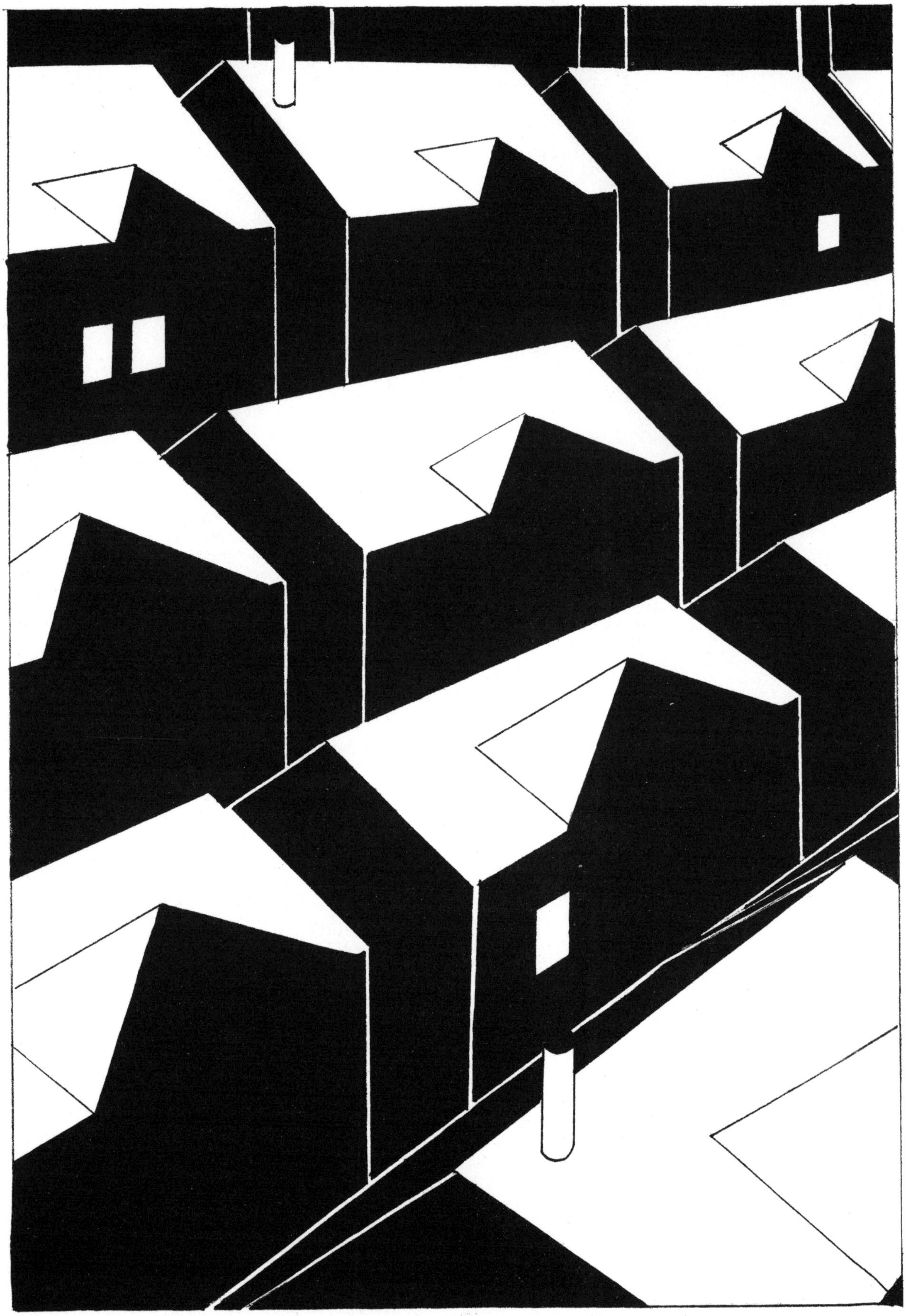

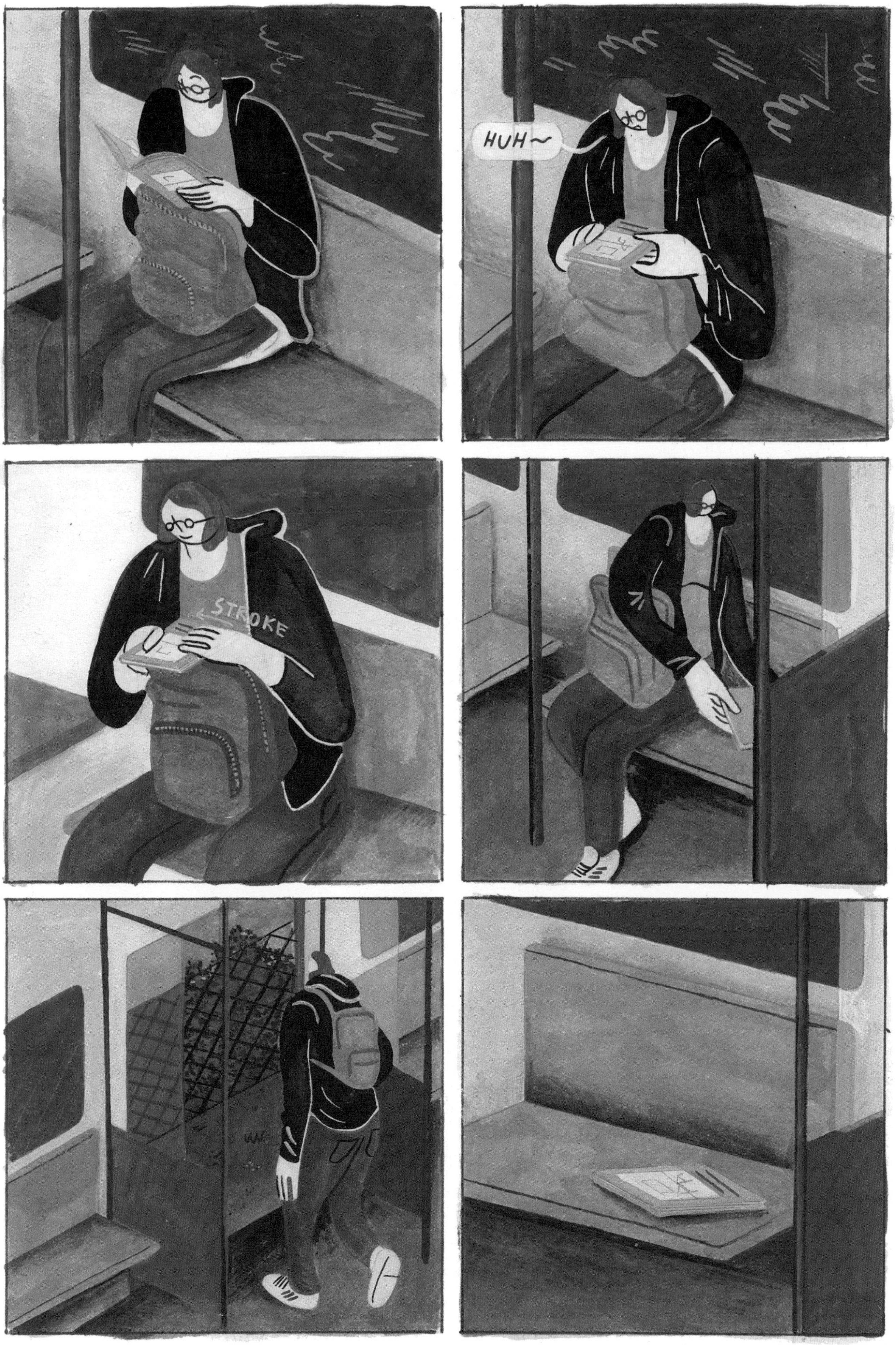
HUH~
STROKE

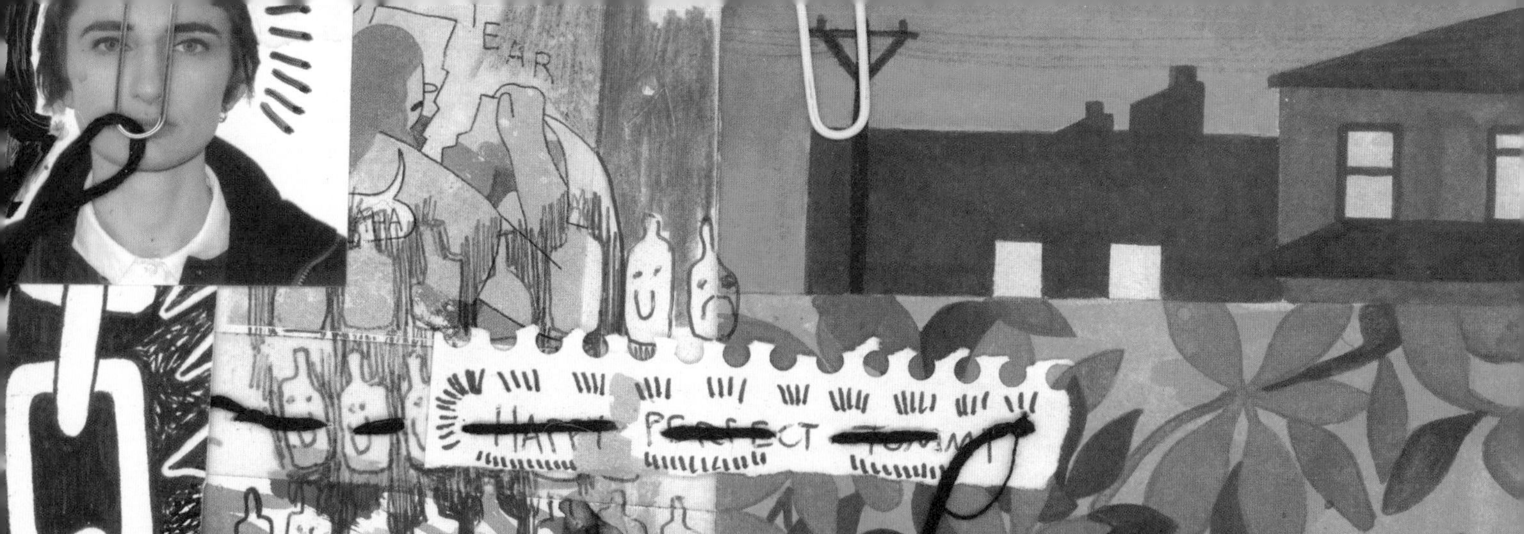

BACK COVER PHOTOS: MORGAN HICKINBOTHAM

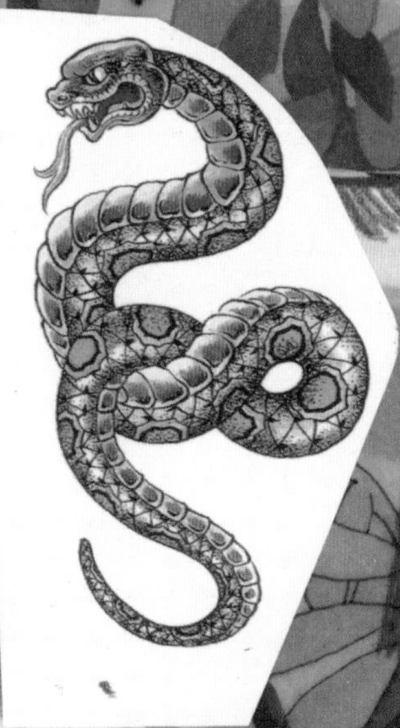

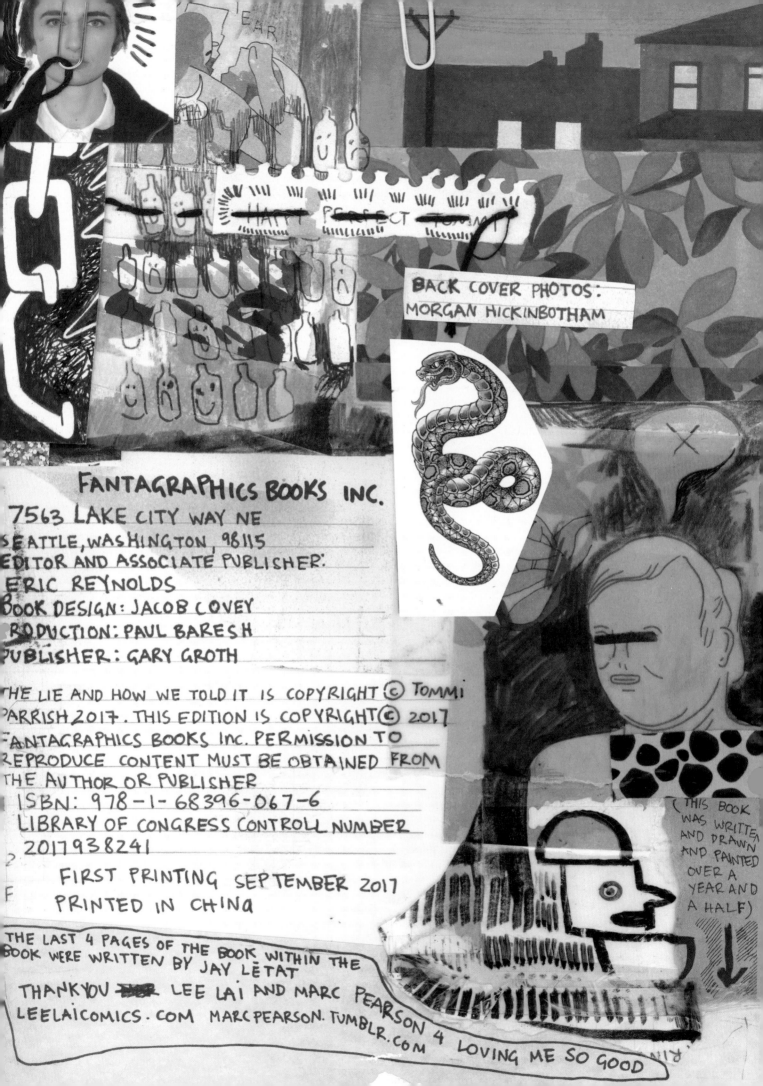

FANTAGRAPHICS BOOKS INC.
7563 LAKE CITY WAY NE
SEATTLE, WASHINGTON, 98115
EDITOR AND ASSOCIATE PUBLISHER: ERIC REYNOLDS
BOOK DESIGN: JACOB COVEY
PRODUCTION: PAUL BARESH
PUBLISHER: GARY GROTH

ISBN: 978-1-68396-067-6
LIBRARY OF CONGRESS CONTROLL NUMBER 2017938241

FIRST PRINTING SEPTEMBER 2017
PRINTED IN CHINA

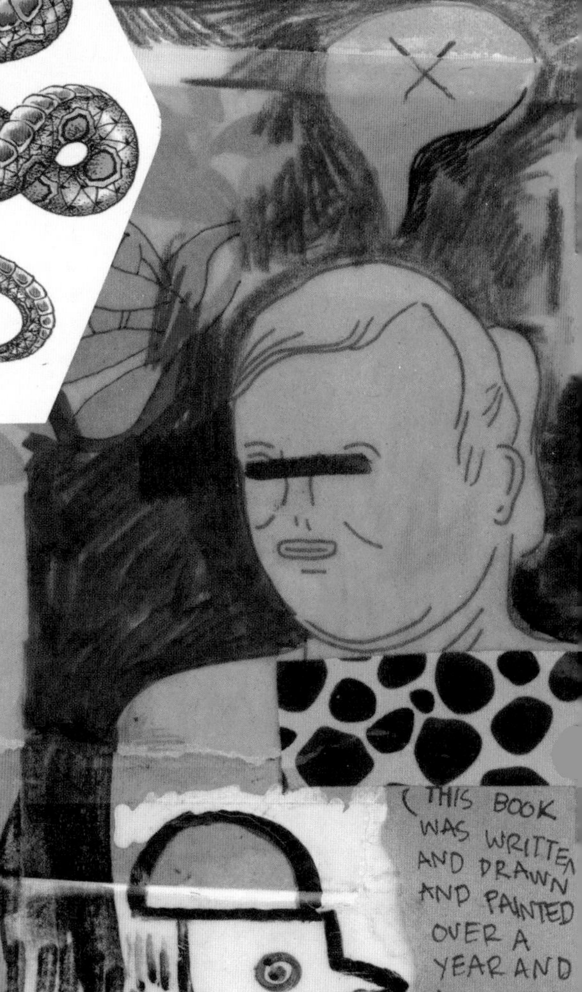

(THIS BOOK WAS WRITTEN AND DRAWN AND PAINTED OVER A YEAR AND A HALF)

THE LAST 4 PAGES OF THE BOOK WITHIN THE BOOK WERE WRITTEN BY JAY LÉTAT

THANKYOU [redacted] LEE LAI AND MARC PEARSON 4 LOVING ME SO GOOD
LEELAICOMICS.COM MARCPEARSON.TUMBLR.COM

TOMMI PARRISH WAS BORN IN MELBOURNE, AUSTRALIA
IN 1989, THEY CURRENTLY LIVE IN MONTREAL IN A HOUSE
WITH TWO DOGS, TWO CATS AND SIX OTHER HUMANS.
TOMMI HAS COMICS IN THE PERMANENT COLLECTION
AT THE GALLERY OF WESTERN AUSTRALIA, HAS A SECOND
BOOK COMING OUT WITH 2DCLOUD AND HAS HAD SHOWS,
DELIVERED WORKSHOPS AND GIVEN TALKS THROUGHOUT
AUSTRALIA, NORTH AMERICA AND ARGENTINA.

THEY SPEND THEIR DAYS PAINTING COMICS AT THE
KITCHEN TABLE.